SHIFT

jennifer bradbury **SHIFT**

Atheneum Books for Young Readers

New York   London   Toronto   Sydney   New Delhi

ATHENEUM BOOKS FOR YOUNG READERS
An imprint of Simon & Schuster Children's Publishing Division
1230 Avenue of the Americas, New York, New York 10020
ATHENEUM BOOKS FOR YOUNG READERS is a registered trademark of Simon & Schuster, Inc.
For information about special discounts for bulk purchases, please contact Simon & Schuster Special Sales at 1-866-506-1949 or business@simonandschuster.com.
The Simon & Schuster Speakers Bureau can bring authors to your live event. For more information or to book an event, contact the Simon & Schuster Speakers Bureau at 1-866-248-3049 or visit our website at www.simonspeakers.com.
Also available in an Atheneum Books for Young Readers hardcover edition
Book design by Mike Rosamilia
The text for this book is set in Meridien.
Manufactured in the United States of America
First Atheneum Books for Young Readers paperback edition April 2012
10 9 8 7 6 5 4 3 2 1
The Library of Congress has cataloged the hardcover edition as follows:
Bradbury, Jennifer
Shift/Jennifer Bradbury.—1st ed.
p. cm.
Summary: When best friends Chris and Win go on a cross-country bicycle trek the summer after graduating and only one returns, the FBI wants to know what happened.
ISBN 978-1-4169-4732-5 (hc)
[1. Bicycles and bicycling—Fiction. 2. Travel—Fiction. 3. Missing persons—Fiction. 4. Best friends—Fiction. 5. Friendship—Fiction.]
1. Title
PZ7.B1643 Sh 2008
[Fic]—dc22 2007023558
ISBN 978-1-4424-0852-4 (pbk)
ISBN 978-1-4424-2012-0 (eBook)

For Jimmy—
always my first,
best,
and favorite reader

SHIFT

ACKNOWLEDGMENTS

Shift's journey has been as challenging and eventful as the one reflected in the story. Like my characters, I'm lucky I didn't have to go it alone. To all the brave travelers who read early (or multiple) drafts of the story, I owe a debt greater than I can repay. Thanks to Troy and Angie Wright, Kyle and Christy Johnson, Joe Vellegas, Jenny Black, Jana and Derry Billingsley, Jules Hargan, Todd Reynolds, Monica and Alex Adkins, June Bradbury, Maryann and Jerry Faughn, Tom Samples, and Andrew and Becky Campbell for pedaling through the uphill climb of the early versions. Thanks to my ninth-grade classes at Burlington-Edison High School for their insightful comments during writing workshops—you've been the best writing teachers and guides I could ask for. Thanks to Bhavan Vidyalya in Chandigarh, India, for providing me space to work (and to Aryan and Vashundara for the welcome distractions). Thanks to Cathy Belben and Laural Ringler for inviting me into the writing life and proving great companions on the journey. Thanks to Robin Rue and the folks at Writers House for their faith and enthusiasm in the story—you showed up at just the right moment. Thanks to Caitlyn Dlouhy, whose vision and insight forced me to find new gears as a writer and, ultimately, made the story what it is now. And although you have no idea what you did, thanks to Evic June for the long afternoon naps and for reminding me what really matters. Finally, to Jimmy for sharing your stories and filling our life with so many. Any journey with you is richer for it—especially this one.

CHAPTER ONE

The nose of the seat bit into my shoulder as the toe clip scraped the back of my thigh. I wrestled the bike through the dorm's gaping front doors, the derailleur cable snagging on the knob as I stepped inside. I lurched, swore, and hoped none of the half-dozen people hanging around the sweltering lobby were watching. I tried to block out the lingering smells of puke and cheap beer as I headed for the row of mailboxes along the far wall.

Through the glass of box number 118, I saw a small scrap of green paper. As I fumbled in my pocket for my box key, the bike slipped off my shoulder and crashed to the tile floor. I swore again, let the bike lay where it fell, and pulled the message out of the mailbox.

TO: *Chris Collins*
FROM: *Your mommy*
RE: *Win*
NOTES: *Call home immediately. Urgent.*

I *had* to start carrying my cell phone. Mom had probably left a couple of messages on it already. She was pretty thorough when she got panicky, and lately she panicked a lot. Part of it was her having a hard time letting go. The other part had more to do with what happened this summer. Still, I couldn't imagine what qualified as urgent these days with her. Had she found another one of my socks in the dryer?

The desk phone rang. Behind the counter another freshman who'd fared better in the work-study lottery than I had answered while managing to keep his gaze on the TV blaring from across the mock living room, a mixture of sweaty tile, cast-off couches, and giant floor fans that had to have been around since the eighties.

"Armstrong Hall," he mumbled as I shut the mailbox, shoved the message and key into my pocket, and heaved my bike back onto my shoulder. But then a voice too close made me jump.

"I hear those things are a lot easier if you ride them instead of letting them ride you," said a man in a dark suit as he gestured toward the bike.

I nodded, looked the guy over. "Chain busted on the way back from the square," I said, wondering why this guy had decided I looked like I was in a mood for conversation. The tie meant he was probably someone's dad.

"Too bad," he said.

I shrugged, causing the bike to slip again, the back wheel banging into the mailboxes. The whole cycling-around-campus thing hadn't turned out to be as cool as I'd imagined. People in the way. Speed bumps. Crowded sidewalks. Stairs.

I missed the road.

"Nice talking to you," I said, taking a step toward the hallway.

"You're Christopher Collins." No hint of a question in his voice.

I answered anyway, taking another look at him as I did so. He must have been at least six feet tall, because I could look him straight in the eyes without slouching, but he had me by forty pounds, easy. Not that that was surprising. I'd been the skinny kid since second grade.

"Yeah?"

"Must have a lot of miles on that thing," he said, pointing toward the chain dangling from the front crank. "They don't wear out fast, do they?"

My legs began to itch from the inside out. For as long as I can remember, the itching has been an early warning indicator. Anytime I have that feeling, I know something big is on the horizon. The sensation is as reliable as the smell of rain before a storm. "Who are you?" I asked.

"Abe Ward," he said, reaching into his breast pocket. The gesture allowed the flap of his jacket to fall open, revealing a slick-looking pistol holstered just above his belt. "I'm with the FBI, based here in Atlanta. Mind if I ask you a few questions?" He pulled his hand out of his pocket and flipped open an ID badge with a practiced motion. His voice was even, measured, his forehead dry even in the oppressive heat.

Anytime somebody wants to ask me a few questions, my natural suspicions come into play. But when that person has a gun and flashes an official-looking piece of government ID, I can only say one thing.

"Shoot." I dropped the bike to the floor and leaned it against the wall.

Mr. Ward actually grinned.

"What's this about?" I asked.

He ignored my question, gesturing toward a couch in a quieter corner of the room. "This okay with you?"

I nodded. "Sure." My roommate, Jati, was an international student from Malaysia. If I brought a guy in a suit with a government ID into the room, he'd probably think someone was coming to revoke his visa.

Ward sat. I sank into a chair across from him. A scarred coffee table littered with old copies of alumni magazines and the student newspaper—the *Technique*—filled the space between us. "You probably know what this is about," he began. Something about the way my legs were itching said I did, but the message hadn't quite reached my brain. I shook my head lamely. Maybe spending the last few days playing getting-to-know-you games and talking about the evils of binge drinking had made me stupid.

"Heard from Win lately?" Ward asked.

Win. Short for Winston. Short for "bane of my existence and onetime best friend."

I tossed my head back against the couch. Great. "Mr. Coggans sent you," I said.

"Answer the question, please," he replied.

I sighed. I wasn't eager to jump back into the events I'd been recounting to Win's parents and mine since I returned without him two weeks ago. I thought once I got to school, I might get a break. Apparently not. "No. Not since I finished the trip—well, sort of finished the trip—with him a couple of weeks ago. We got separated at the end, and I couldn't find him. So I rode to the coast, got on a bus, and came home. Showed up here for orientation a week after that."

"Why didn't you look for him after you reached the coast?" the agent asked.

Besides the fact that he didn't bother looking for me? I thought. "I figured he'd gone on to his uncle's in Seattle." Truth was, I was still pissed at him for not stopping when I got that flat near Concrete, Washington, a dead little town fifty miles from the coast.

"Why didn't you go to Seattle?"

"Win never told me the address. Or the phone number. Or even his uncle's name," I said.

Ward pressed on. "But I'm sure there were other ways you could have gotten the information—"

"Probably. But I was a little tired of it all by then," I said.

"Tired of what?" he asked, his voice inching from the friendly tone he'd opened with to something more businesslike.

"Win's always playing games. I was sick of him. Getting to Seattle would have been too much of a hassle."

"Doesn't seem like a guy who'd ridden his bike across the

country would have minded. What can it be, an eighty-mile ride?"

"That's a whole day of riding, and probably more since I'd have been on back roads. We only rode freeways when we had to."

"Didn't the bus stop in Seattle before it turned back east?" he asked.

I nodded. "For maybe half an hour."

He paused, scratched the back of his head. "Why didn't you call Win's parents when you split up?"

I shrugged. "I was in the middle of nowhere. And Win had the cell phone. But that was dead by then. Besides, it didn't seem right that since Win decided to ride on his own, I should be the one to catch hell for it."

"Huh," he said finally.

"What's going on with Win?" I'd been telling myself for the last week that he must have turned up, since his dad had stopped making his daily phone calls. It dawned on me that if the FBI was involved, then that could mean a lot of things . . . few of them good for Win . . . or me.

Again he ignored my question. "But you could have called them to get the uncle's address."

I hesitated. Since middle school I'd avoided conversations with Win's parents almost as carefully as Win did himself, but I didn't want to go into all that. "Seattle's a pretty big place. Why won't you tell me what's going on?"

The agent stared at me a little longer; I tried to stare back, was reminded of the stupid contests Win and I used to engage in, and looked away.

Ward began to loosen his tie, as if he knew we might be here awhile. "Do you want to try that again?"

"What?" I asked.

"That story."

"It's the truth," I said, sounding more panicked than I wanted to.

He shook his head. "Nope."

I was taken aback.

"You're kidding, right? Why would I lie?" I couldn't remember the last time someone had accused me of lying.

He glared at me again. I wonder if the feds provide training for intimidating stares at the FBI academy. Or maybe it's a prerequisite—like running a six-minute mile. His gaze made me so uncomfortable that I began to doubt my own story.

"I told the exact same thing to my folks when I got on the bus to come back," I said.

"Yeah. I talked with them earlier today."

He'd talked to my parents? "So then you know I'm telling the truth, right?"

Ward snorted. "Nope. I only know that you lie consistently. This isn't high school PE—a note from your mommy isn't going to get you out of climbing the rope."

"What exactly is 'this'?" I asked, almost as annoyed by another mama's-boy reference as I was freaked by the appearance of an FBI agent asking me questions about something I'd been trying pretty damn hard to forget.

"*This*," Ward said, "is an investigation."

"Of what?" I asked. "Me?"

Ward was quiet for a beat. The fans droned heavily behind me.

On TV the announcer shouted, "Yahtzee!" as a player smacked the ball out of the park on the highlight reel.

"Win *has* no uncle in Seattle," he said carefully, gauging my reaction. "And he hasn't contacted his parents in over a month. You're the last person to have seen him."

Shit.

"I think you'd better start from the beginning, Chris," Abe Ward said as he settled back into the sofa, one arm tossed casually across the back so I had a better view of the weapon sleeping quietly in its holster.

CHAPTER TWO

Three weeks before I graduated from high school my mother asked me a question. Actually, Mom never really asked anything, she just camouflaged commands inside queries.

"Wouldn't you like to get a job this summer, Chris?" Translation: "You're too old to sit around here all summer mooching money off your father and me."

"I mean, you'll want to have spending money for college next fall, right?"

I hadn't even decided if I was going to college yet. The acceptance letter and my housing application for Georgia Tech were still in my backpack, wedged between wave theory and relativity in my AP physics textbook—a fitting spot for a decision I'd yet to make.

"Mom . . ."

"Kmart's hiring. You'd like working there, wouldn't you?"

Generally talking about me getting a job was one thing, but she'd clearly been making plans. I had an immediate and horrifying vision of myself wearing a stupid plastic name tag and one of those lower-back support belts as I unloaded giant boxes of toilet paper destined for Blue Light Specials.

The thought of a summer spent shuffling two-ply for the value-minded made me desperate. And I did sort of have other plans. Plans I'd so far been too chicken to share with anyone but Win.

"Actually . . . I'm going to ride my bike to the West Coast with Win," I said.

Mom blinked. "West Coast? West Coast of what?"

My father, who had just come into the kitchen, tossed his lunch box in the sink and said, "Sounds good, Chris. Make sure you call once in a while." He tried to sound casual, but instead of emptying his lunch box and loading the mason jar he used as a thermos into the dishwasher, he leaned against the counter and looked at me, his eyes filled with a weird blend of admiration and crazy hope.

"Now hold on," my mother said, regaining her composure. "Shouldn't we discuss this?" I could see her regretting the early graduation present—a rebuilt Trek 1200—they'd given me a few weeks back. Sure, Abby Sanders got a new 4Runner, but I wasn't complaining. The road bike fit. Win and I had been entering biathlons since freshman year. I'd been limping to decent finishes on a pathetic ten-speed my dad found at a flea market. This bike would fly. It begged to.

Saying out loud that I was going to ride across the country and seeing that nobody laughed gave me confidence. It *was* as crazy as it sounded, but it was within the realm of possibility. If it weren't, Mom wouldn't have been so worried.

"Win and I have been talking about it," I said. That wasn't technically true. A few months ago we'd been sitting around watching the Discovery Channel on a Friday night because . . . well, because we really were that lame. They ran a documentary about this guy who rode his bike from somewhere in Europe all the way down to the bottom of Africa. One of us said, "Wouldn't it be cool to ride our bikes out west?" Win and I hadn't so much as discussed it since, but the notion had sustained me through the most debilitating later stages of senioritis.

But Mom was not to be denied her discussion. "The West Coast is a long way from West Virginia. Probably at least two thousand miles," she said.

"Closer to three, I'd imagine," my father said, sounding excited. I wasn't exactly surprised at his reaction, but maybe a little at his enthusiasm. He'd had moments that made me wonder if he hadn't been a hell-raiser before he got married, built this house, and started moving heavy stuff around for a living. When I built a tiny ramp on the flat part of the driveway for that five-horsepower minibike I got one Christmas, he was the one who squirted a thin line of lighter fluid and laid a match to it when I came tearing around the house to jump it again. This felt a little like that.

Mom shot him a *Don't encourage the boy* look. "Maybe you could just ride to Gram's house." Gram's house was in Ohio, a three-hour drive away. Not *out west*.

"It has to be farther. The whole point is to see something different," I argued.

She sat back and crossed her arms. "This is Win's idea, isn't it? You know I couldn't love that boy any more if he were my own, but his greatest talent is getting you into trouble."

"Mom—," I began.

"Remember the tree house incident? Or that time at school you got blamed when he decided to change those letters around on the bulletin board and made you stand watch?"

"That was fifth grade, Mom," I said, adding, "*I* want to do this."

"What about last fall when you guys went for your campus visit at Marshall?"

She waited for me to argue. But the mention of the Marshall Plan, as Win had called it then, threatened to make me laugh out loud—something I was sure Mom wouldn't appreciate in this conversation.

"Remember those outlandish lies?" she said, arms crossed as she stared at me across the table.

"Mom, that was just Win goofing around—"

"He told that poor student tour guide that you'd been in a coma for three years!"

"Mom—" I tried to break in, but I could feel the smile pulling at the corners of my mouth.

"I'm not finished, Christopher," she intoned. I shut up and let her continue. "And he wasn't satisfied with just that lie, was he?"

I sat quietly, unsure if I was supposed to answer this question or not.

"Um, no, but—"

"He went on to tell her that he was an orphan refugee from—" She paused, waved her fingers toward me, beckoning the answer.

"I don't remember, Mom. One of the Stan countries, maybe?"

But it didn't matter. Now she only wanted to ensure this was as long and painful as possible. *"And,"* she said, positively vibrating as she said the words, "and he claimed to be your adopted brother who'd tutored you to make up for those years of high school you missed during your coma!"

My father laughed. "It's not funny, Allen!" Mom said. "Chris could have gotten a lot of scholarship money at Marshall. And then he would have been close to home instead of going all the way down to Atlanta."

"I didn't even apply to Marshall, Mom," I said.

Mom glowered. "Of course not! As if you could after I had to explain to the dean that Win made it all up."

She shook her head at the memory. "I don't think I've ever been so humiliated. That nice man pulling me out of a parent meeting to tell me personally how much he admired the sacrifices I'd made for my sons."

"At least you got to be the hero in that one," I said. "All I got to be was a coma survivor."

"And which exactly do you think you'll be after this little adventure with Win?" she snapped, referring to the bike trip.

"This is totally different."

She settled down some, tried a different approach. "Really?

Because I don't think even you have enough faith in that boy to leave the details to him. Besides, how do you even ride a bike that far? Where will you live?"

"We'll camp."

"How will you pay for it?"

"I've got some money saved. Between graduation gifts and all the lawns I mowed this spring, I have enough."

"But it's irresponsible—," she began before my father cut her off.

"Of course it is. Chris is plenty responsible. Did better than either of us in school. Took all those hard classes. Got accepted into college. He works hard."

"Allen, we—"

"He deserves this trip. He's got a whole life of responsibility ahead of him. Let him have a season of . . . of . . ."

"Irresponsibility?" my mother supplied, sounding satisfied.

"Fun," my father said. "Adventure."

Something in his tone and the way he looked sort of past my mother as he said it was definitive. But Mom had one last line of defense. "Well, I suppose if Winston's parents say it's all right."

She was of course hoping Win's parents—famous for their unflinching ability to dampen all things fun or irresponsible— would strike down the spirit of adventure. In truth, I expected the same.

But they didn't. At least not fatally.

When I called that night, Win picked up on the third or fourth ring. "What?"

"It's me," I said.

"Yeah, Collins, I have caller ID. And considering this is a private line and you're the only person who calls me besides telemarketers or people who think they're calling my dad's number—"

"Dude, I get it. What's your problem?"

He sighed. "Apparently it's still got something to do with authority or attachment or some crap like that. I can't remember what it is this week."

"Therapy today?" I asked.

"Yeah."

"Oh."

"Yeah," he said again after a moment, while I looked for something to say.

When I still couldn't think of anything wise, I went for the obvious. "Go ask your parents if you can do the ride this summer," I said, explaining my dad's encouragement and Mom's grudging permission.

I heard Win open his bedroom door and head down the hallway. "They really said yes?"

"Sort of," I said. "Do you think your dad will go for it?"

"Maybe. The stock report's on now."

We were lucky the stocks were on. Lucky something more important than Win's safety and happiness could provide the distraction. The plasma TV in the den grew louder as Win approached his father's domain, the phone still in his hand.

A quiet knock at the door. The volume dropping on the TV a little.

"Hey, Dad?"

"What is it, Winston?" I heard his father ask, followed by the sound of an ice cube clinking against the bottom of a glass as his father tossed back the remains of what I knew was his after-work scotch.

"Uh, Chris and I want to ride our bikes cross-country this summer," he said.

The hum of the television was the only sound for a few seconds.

"I see," his father said.

"His parents already said it's okay," Win said.

"That sounds pretty ambitious," he said, adding, "especially for you."

I guess I thought that since this trip was something special that maybe Win's dad wouldn't be the prick he usually was when Win asked him about something. I was wrong, and I found myself sort of shrinking the way I did when Win's dad laid into him in front of me. Too afraid to move or leave or anything that might make it worse for Win or give his dad a reason to look at me like he looked at Win—as if I were somebody he wanted to fire rather than a kid. I thought about hanging up, but it felt too much like leaving Win alone in there with his dad.

"Dad?" I heard Win say again.

His father spoke above the fake exciting music accompanying the listings. "I suppose if Chris's parents allow it, I'll let you try. Though don't expect us to jump in the car and come bail you out when you get bored of this adventure after a week or so."

Win said something I couldn't make out as the volume grew louder.

"We're good," he then said into the phone. "Dad seems pretty stoked, but that might have been the scotch talking."

Since no one technically gave us permission, we never actually repeated the exact phrases to each other's parents. We just started telling people that we were going to do it, making Seattle our destination because Win had an uncle there we could stay with.

We lived in that mode—the glory of the adventure to come—for a full week without making any concrete plans. Then my dad sat me down on the back porch after I'd reminded Mom that I was going to ride my bike across the country instead of get a job (a declaration prompted by the fact that she'd brought home an application from KFC).

My dad's a man of few words—and those allotted to me throughout my lifetime have always seemed to mean more.

"Son," he began.

"Nice start, Obi-Wan," I joked. "But remember, you gave me the talk years ago, and it still hasn't done me any good—"

"Son, when I was twenty-one, before I married your mother, I planned to drive Route 66 from Chicago to California in a '67 Mustang I restored," he said, the last phrase falling with uncharacteristic wistfulness.

I shut up.

"Talked about it for two years. Even overhauled the engine a couple of times."

I focused on the gap between the decking boards, a screw whose head had been stripped out. Anything to avoid seeing on his face what I could hear in his voice: regret.

"But I just talked. Never committed. Never cleared my life

out enough to start driving. Kept thinking I'd save a little more, get a few things taken care of. Then I met your mom."

I nodded. Less because I understood, and more because I wanted this conversation to end.

"Set a date, Chris," he finished with an urgency I hadn't heard in his voice since, well, since maybe never.

"Set a date and leave—no matter what," he repeated. He stood, signaling the end of the one-sided exchange. I nodded. He turned and entered the house, leaving me with the revelation that my dad—who'd spent the last twenty-two years working construction and dreaming about a long drive—*needed* me to go on this trip.

The cicadas chirped in the trees, echoing the buzzing that had begun in my legs. What had started out as a fun way to spend a summer dodging minimum wage had become a quest. I stood, took two steps across the deck, tugged open the creaking screen door, and reached for the phone.

Win answered on the second ring.

"June sixth," I said.

"Foxtrot," he shot back.

I wasn't sure how to respond.

"Code, right? We're speaking in code or something?" he said, sounding bored.

"Does June sixth sound like code?"

"Nope. Sounds like the day after graduation. Sounds like I might be hungover."

"Don't be. We'll probably put in seventy miles, and I don't plan to stop so you can hurl," I said.

"Come on, man. The seventh would be better. Lucky and all—," he began before I cut him off.

"The sixth," I said.

He sighed. "Whatever. Roger . . . or something."

I hung up, picked up a pen emblazoned with the name of my parents' bank, and wrote CHRIS & WIN LEAVE in careful block letters on the calendar.

My mother walked in bearing a load of folded laundry.

"What's that?" she asked, gesturing toward the date I'd been filling in on the calendar.

"A promise," I said, capping the pen and tucking it back into the mug on the counter before I headed to my room.

CHAPTER THREE

"That's not possible," I said, shaking my head. "His uncle was always part of the plan."

Ward paused for a second. "What's his name?" he asked.

"What?"

"The uncle. His name."

I stared at the FBI agent. "I can't remember," I said, suddenly wondering if the reason I couldn't was because Win never told me. Suddenly remembering how his parents looked at me the first time I mentioned Win's uncle. The one Win made up. His father's eyes narrowed, his mother's widened in confusion, and she started to say something before Coggans placed a hand on her knee. She stopped immediately.

"If he doesn't have an uncle in Seattle, why didn't his parents say so? I must have mentioned it a hundred times last week when we met with them."

Ward reached for the back of his neck, rubbed a spot behind his ear, and looked past me in a way that told me he wasn't about to answer my question. "Whose idea was it to take this trip?"

"Nobody's. Both of ours. We sort of both took credit for it when the other wasn't listening."

He rolled his eyes.

"Look, Win and I have been friends since third grade. Best friends since about sixth. At one point we sorta started sharing a brain," I said. "The trip idea more just *happened* to both of us at once."

"So how come that shared brain didn't clue you in that Win was lying?"

I shrugged. "I don't know. Win lied about a lot of stuff. A lot."

"But you never thought to check on the Seattle thing?" he asked me.

I shook my head, suddenly feeling stupid. "Guess I never thought he'd lie about something so obvious."

Ward made a face and shook his head slightly from side to side in a way that reminded me of my history teacher from tenth grade when somebody said something boneheaded in class.

"I don't know what to tell you," I said.

"Where's Win?" he asked me.

"I have no idea."

"Tell me again why you didn't call Win's parents when you got separated?"

Pick a reason. After 3,200 miles of riding, Win had done more than enough to piss me off. I was done being his Boy Scout. Was it my problem that his folks had finally managed to muster up something resembling concern for their only kid? "I was mad, I guess."

"Mad?" He grabbed that one out of the air in a hurry. "As in angry?"

"Not like that," I backpedaled. "Look, what do they think happened to Win?"

"We're going to find out, Christopher," he said. "Trouble is, right now the only person who can tell us anything at all about Win's disappearance is you. And this whole Seattle story? Not making you look too hot."

"What, do Win's parents think *I* did something to him?" I asked. They didn't like me any more than they did Win, but the fact that they thought, what, that I'd hurt him or something, made me feel sort of ill. Granted, if anybody had motive, it would have been me. I'd actually entertained some pretty morbid thoughts after he left me alone on the side of the road. But I'd never have done anything like . . . like whatever Ward was suggesting.

But just because I hadn't hurt him didn't mean someone else hadn't. Or that he hadn't been hit by a car. Or attacked by something . . . or any of the scenarios my mother had cycled through during the week I was home, between the trip and coming to school. I was pretty sure Win had just bailed, but even copping to that much to anyone—my parents, his, or now Ward—made me feel sick for another reason.

"They don't know what to think," he said. "They haven't spoken with their son since he left."

"But he called them every week!" I said.

Ward shook his head. "Win left phone messages for the first six weeks. He stopped leaving them a couple of weeks before he disappeared."

Something else they forgot to tell me last week when they'd grilled me after I returned without Win. Then again, they'd never corrected me when I mentioned the uncle in Seattle, so apparently there was a lot they didn't tell us, a lot they didn't want us to know they'd overlooked.

His mom *had* spent plenty of time complaining that they should have been able to reach us by cell phone. We'd packed Win's because both sets of parents insisted we keep it for emergencies, but Win went swimming with it in his jersey pocket on, like, the third day and shorted out the insides. We knew we'd get an earful about responsibility and safety and all that if we told them what had happened, so we just made lame excuses about not getting reception along the back roads we were following. The only help in an emergency it might have been would have relied on our throwing it hard enough at whoever was trying to mug us. Truth was, I never wanted to feel like anybody from home could reach us whenever they wanted. Win had even more reason.

"As far as I knew, he was calling them every week. We'd find a set of pay phones every Sunday and call in," I said.

Ward shrugged. "Win left messages. His parents managed to miss every call."

"They never said anything to my parents or me," I said. "My mom would have gotten me to make Win call them at work or something."

"He hasn't spoken to either of them in more than two and a half months," Ward reiterated.

"And it only took 'em that long to get concerned," I muttered.

"What was that?" Ward asked.

"Nothing," I said, popping to my feet. My legs were going crazy. "Can I ask a question?" I didn't wait for a response. "Why are you the first legal-type person I've talked to? I mean, we've all been talking with Win's parents and stuff, but I haven't heard from them for a week, and I sort of figured that meant Win had come home after he got bored doing whatever he was doing. Isn't jumping straight to the FBI, well, a little much?"

He leaned forward and rested his elbows on his knees, let his hands dangle to the floor between them. He looked like a folding table collapsed in the wrong position. "Missing persons is federal jurisdiction. I have a good reputation," he said simply.

It struck me that he was actually being less honest with me than I was with him, though I was the one under suspicion.

"And his folks are trying to keep it quiet?" I supplied.

Ward nodded. "When he didn't show up at home in time to go to his orientation at Dartmouth, well, they didn't want to let on that he was missing. Seems Win just barely got in, his father had to pull a few strings . . . and if he blows this shot . . ." He trailed off. "Let's just say his folks want to get him home."

I laughed. "Sounds like them. Win would have enjoyed the fact they were squirming in the face of the precious Ivy League."

"Interesting choice of words," he said, rubbing his temples.

I panicked. "Look, I only meant if he were here to watch it, not like he's . . . you know."

"You sure you haven't heard from him?" he asked again.

"Positive."

He rose to leave, fished a business card out of his wallet, and handed it to me. "I'll be back Monday—around this time."

"Classes start Monday," I said, though I knew it wouldn't help.

He shot me another stare. "Enjoy your weekend, Mr. Collins," he said, heading for the door.

A thought occurred to me. Curiosity got the better of good sense. "What do you owe him?" I asked. "Him" was Winston's father.

Ward paused in the doorway, dropped his chin, but didn't turn back to face me. "Small favor for a friend," he said. "That's all."

And then I knew I'd guessed right. Win's father didn't have any friends.

CHAPTER FOUR

"Tell me again why we're here?"
I asked. We'd taken our last high school final yesterday and had
the day off today. Graduation practice was this afternoon. Somehow
the school got away with requiring the senior class to go to the
wave pool on the day before graduation every year. But Win fed
Principal Keller two ridiculous lies: He had a life-threatening
chlorine allergy, and I was suffering post-traumatic stress disorder
brought about by witnessing my cousin's drowning at a waterslide
park. I'm pretty sure Keller would have bought any lie as long as
it meant he didn't have to chaperone Win. He just ordered us to
be back on campus by four for practice.

The lies were justified, though; we really needed time to finish
preparing for the trip. But this detour to his father's office wasn't

part of the plan. "My dad left a note telling me to come by," he said, turning without warning down a short hallway that ended with a frosted glass door flanked by two fake ferns standing in planters.

"Why?" I asked.

Win shrugged. "Dunno. I'm trying to keep from pissing him off so he can't change his mind about the trip, but if you want to demand answers from the guy, be my guest."

I shut up as he pushed open the glass door and we found ourselves in a large waiting room lined with leather couches studded by brass rivets, and bookshelves bearing various award plaques and three-ring binders, spines all clearly labeled and turned the same way. A woman in a yellow dress sat at a small desk next to a heavy wooden door bearing a brass plate etched with Win's father's name and title.

"Hello, Winston," she said. "Mr. Coggans will be with you in a moment. His ten o'clock ran long." Her smile failed just a bit as Win's dad yelled a little louder at whomever he had locked in his office with him. Win nodded and slid onto one of the leather sofas a few feet away, picking up a crisp copy of *Newsweek* and flipping straight to the editorial cartoon pages.

"How come there are no windows in here?" I whispered to Win.

He looked up, surveyed the oaken paneled walls and paintings of warships on stormy seas. "You saw what we drove through," he said, adding, "This way management can at least pretend they're not working in the middle of a chemical manufacturing plant."

I'd seen the smokestacks and acres of holding tanks of Titan

Chemical from the freeway during countless trips up to Charleston. But I'd never even been off the exit here, much less to Coggans's office. What was amazing was that I was surprised to find that the tang of chemicals was stronger sitting in Win's car on the freeway outside than it was in here.

Before I could ask how they managed that, the door to the inner office opened.

"I'm sorry for the misunderstanding, Mr. Coggans," said a man in a pin-striped suit who looked familiar. Like I'd seen him in a commercial or something on TV.

"You've always been a friend to Titan, Senator," Win's father said, extending his hand to his guest as I gaped. Grayson Samples had just won reelection last fall to his post in Washington. Now he was sweating and looking like he might piddle on the floor. "I know you'll take care of this."

I leaned over to Win and said quietly, "What the hell? Your dad's been screaming at a senator?"

"Better him than me," Win said without looking up.

"Who gets a senator to come to his office?" I said, staring at the two men like they were a traffic accident on the freeway. I couldn't seem to look away.

"My dad," Win said as we watched Samples hasten for the door. Win's father turned to us. "Boys," he said, nodding and stepping back into his office, leaving the door open for us to follow.

"Our turn," said Win as we rose from the couch, then hurried around the table and across the waiting room.

Win's father's office was even bigger than the waiting room.

One wall held a row of windows up high near the ceiling, but the frosted glass blocked the view of smokestacks spewing fumes into the air. Mr. Coggans walked to the other side of a desk that was easily the size of my bedroom, and opened a drawer.

"Winston," he said, "come here."

Win walked over while I hung near the doorway. Mr. Coggans pulled a slip of paper from the drawer and held it out to Win.

"What's this?" he asked.

"Your graduation present," his father said.

"Oh," Win said, and then after looking at the check, said, "Oh," again.

"Tomorrow's going to be rather full, and I may be a bit late to the ceremony, so I thought we could take care of this today," he said.

"Thanks," Win said, sounding as surprised as I felt that his dad was actually acting like a human being.

"You're to buy a new bike with that," he said.

Win looked up sharply. "What?"

"You heard me. I've already had my secretary call the shop in Town Center. They assure me they have the best possible bike for your needs."

Even though he was being a little controlling, it was still a nice gesture.

"Dad, that's cool, but I already have a bike. And Chris and I have been doing a lot of work to get them ready. It takes time to prep for something like this—"

"Go get the bike," he said, sitting down and turning to his computer. "I won't allow you to blame your failure on faulty

29

equipment. If you have the best, then when you don't make it, you'll be forced to deal with the real reason why."

If I hadn't known Win better, I wouldn't have seen his shoulders fall the way they did, the way he fought to keep his hands steady. But I knew him.

"Yeah," he said after a beat. "Good thinking."

His father said nothing more, just reached for the phone and began dialing a number. He was already ripping into someone else as we closed the door softly behind us and quickly crossed the outer office. In the hallway outside I hung back a little as I followed Win through the maze of corridors back to the parking lot. When we could see the haze of the morning sunshine filtering through whatever the plant was refining today, he stopped and looked down at the check in his hand. He stared at it for a second, shook his head softly, and then folded it once.

Then he folded it again.

And again.

And again.

He kept folding until it was so small and so thick that he couldn't make it bend anymore. Then he stepped over to a trash can beside a water fountain and carefully dropped it in, watching it fall.

"Win—," I said.

He looked up at me. "We've got stuff to do, man," he said. "Let's get back to your place."

Neither of us mentioned the check again. Though I wondered how much money Win had just thrown away, I didn't wonder why he'd done it.

By the time we'd swung by the little bike shop back in St. Albans to grab extra tubes, things were beginning to feel normal again. After a run through Taco Bell before returning to my house, I'd convinced myself he'd forgotten about the whole thing. Now he was talking without making much sense and allowing me to do all the work. Both signs indicated that he'd returned to equilibrium.

"C'mon, man, be a pal," Win said.

"No way," I said. "My dad loves those pipes."

"He'll never miss it! He's got, like, nine of the same corncob jobs here on the wall." Win gestured toward a hanger on the Peg-Board above the bench, holding half a dozen of the pipes, all smelling faintly of cherry tobacco.

"You don't even smoke," I said, adding, "and it probably wouldn't be a good idea to start when we're trying to cover eighty miles a day."

"I don't want to smoke it, genius," he said.

"Then, why take it? Every little bit of weight counts."

"I'm not the one drilling holes in my toothbrush handle to save ounces," he said.

"No, you're the one wanting to take useless crap on the road. What do you want it for, anyway?"

He shrugged. "Reminds me of this place."

Before I could ask why he needed to be reminded of my garage, my mom's car pulled up in the driveway. She stopped short of her normal parking spot when she beheld our base camp.

"Don't you think you and Win should work on your bikes in

the barn?" she asked/ordered as she climbed out of the car. There
was no way she could fit her Honda into the garage. The slab floor
was littered with our two bikes, the four sets of saddlebags, and an
impossible amount of camping gear. We were two days away from
departure, had graduation practice in a couple of hours, and had
yet to load the bikes to get the weight balanced.

"Mrs. Collins, we would, but you know I have those nasty dust
allergies," said Win as he helped himself to another handful of
the Spanish peanuts my father kept on his workbench. Win
enjoyed needling my mother—probably because no matter what
he did to his own, she barely reacted.

Mom wasn't playing along today. "What's this?" she
demanded, picking up a jar of peanut butter and holding it like
it was exhibit A in a bad TV courtroom drama.

"The number one brand that moms and kids all love," Win
deadpanned.

The vein on her temple began to pulse. "I mean, what's it doing
here? I bought this jar yesterday," she said. "Isn't the whole point
of your little adventure to be independent?"

My mother ate nothing with any amount of fat in it, and my
father had been having the same turkey sandwich for lunch every
day for the past twenty years. I was the only one who ate peanut
butter.

"I'll pay you for it, if that's what you want," I offered, trying to
sound patient.

"That's not the point. If you're so determined to live on your
own for the next two months, maybe you need to buy your own
groceries?"

This was not about peanut butter. Even so, I couldn't keep the edge out of my voice when I replied, "I know how to buy groceries, Mom."

"And I make excellent lists," Win piped in.

We both ignored him. "Seriously, Mom," I said. "If it's that big a deal, I'll just use it now for the packing and put it back later."

She shook her head, put the jar back on the pile next to my journal and compass, and turned to go.

"Keep it," she said as she left the garage, half slamming the door behind her. The tools above the bench rattled against their hangers in the aftershock. I closed my eyes and tried to remind myself that this woman had a right to give me a hard time. A right to miss me before I'd even gone.

"You know—deep down—she must really like peanut butter," Win said, grinning.

I grabbed a couple of tie-downs and started strapping my sleeping bag and pad to my rear rack, not replying.

"That or she's still not super comfortable with the idea of her baby boy riding his bike in traffic for the next two months."

Still I said nothing, yanking harder on the straps.

"Nah," he said. "It's got to be the peanut butter thing. She must sneak it after-hours, like those ladies in the Lifetime movies. Remember that one we saw—"

"Are you going to help me with this or not?" I asked. Win was still popping back peanuts, elbows perched on the bench.

"I *am* helping," he said. "I'm providing much-needed clarity into the messy domestic situations of your troubled household."

"Don't do that." "That" was Win's favorite pastime of channeling the therapists his parents had been sending him to for the last six years. They couldn't figure out what was wrong with their kid, but wouldn't bother to talk to him when they could pay someone else to. I was the only one who knew about these sessions, and thus the only one who got subjected to his recycled brand of psychobabble. Win wasn't disturbed. He was just a jackass. And a little bored.

He pushed away from the bench and picked up the West Virginia/Ohio map. "You're better at all that, dude. Figure out how to load it best, and I'll learn to repack," he said, unfolding the map and looking at the line I'd highlighted across Highway 60. "Don't your grandparents live in Ohio?"

"Yeah. Free food and a place to crash."

"Works for me," he said, wadding the map back into something like its original shape. I resisted the urge to snatch it from his hands and fold it properly. Years of Win's secondhand therapy had taught me a thing or two about enabling. I'd just fix it after he'd gone.

"Get your money yet?" I asked.

"Tomorrow," he said. "I swear."

I rolled my eyes. Win's dad was worth roughly the gross domestic product of a small island nation, and his mom routinely chucked handfuls of guilt money at my friend. Still, he had a nasty habit of not paying his way. "I'm not letting you bum off me for the next sixty days, Win."

He shook his head sadly. "This from the man who steals Jif from his own, sweet mother."

"Screw you," I said, smiling, as Win tossed a peanut into his mouth, only to have it ricochet off his front tooth.

"Blah, blah, blah, best days of our lives, oh the places we'll go, don't ever change," mumbled Tracy Finn in a parody of the valedictory address that she would deliver tomorrow night. We sat under a giant plastic tent on the football field at the school, grateful for a chance to sit after an hour of marching practice in which even the school band seemed to grow bored.

"Why are we practicing graduation?" Win asked.

"Because apparently marching is *really* hard. And they don't want anybody looking stupid," I said.

"A little redundant, don't you think? Most of us are pretty practiced up on the not falling down and making asses of ourselves. You don't survive this place otherwise," he said.

Win sat beside me. For the last nine years he'd been sitting beside me. In third grade, when his family moved to West Virginia from New York, the teacher labeled our desks in alphabetical order, placing Coggans next to Collins. And things sort of took, because we'd been inseparable right up through senior year. Best friends by default. Tomorrow night I'd follow him as we marched in, follow him as we walked up to get our diplomas. I just hoped I could lead once in a while out on the road.

"Did you get the water filter?" he asked me.

I nodded. "And the iodine tablets."

"Good Eagle," Win said soothingly. Three months ago I'd earned my Eagle Scout rank. Win quit Scouts in eighth grade, but since then he had been mildly harassing me about the fact that I had stayed in. It was one of the items on a long list of things that had started to get old in our friendship.

Down front the guidance counselor took control of the microphone. "Now, don't forget to forget the following items for tomorrow's evening of pomp and circumstance: beach balls, Silly String, air horns, fireworks . . ."

"Well, we don't know how far we'll go between water sources. Some days it might be sixty or seventy miles," I said.

"Stop trying to scare me, Eagle," Win began before Alicia Bivins, who was seated in front of us, text-messaging someone on her cell phone, whirled around to face us.

"You guys are really going to do that bike-ride thingie?" she asked.

I wasn't sure what to say. In fact, I was shocked she'd noticed at all. Alicia—whose looks virtually guaranteed her a spot as the token hot girl on some future reality show—ran in circles decidedly above Chrisandwin.

Win sat up a little straighter. "Hell, yeah."

"No way! So, like, where are you gonna live?"

It was weird that Alicia, who had once publicly humiliated Win in seventh grade when he asked her to the May Day Dance, had deigned us worthy of her attentions.

"Camping in a tent, under the stars, wherever," Win said, sounding cavalier.

"That's so cool," Alicia said. "Wish I could do that."

"Come with us," Win said.

Not that I actually believed that Alicia was any more interested in camping than she was in, well, *us*, but Win's open invite freaked me out a little. Chrisandwinandalicia? Not a chance.

"Yeah, right," she said. "My parents would kill me. Plus, I haven't ridden a bike since, like, middle school." She uttered the last sentence without trying to hide her disgust.

At that moment Dave Anders, who was sitting another row ahead, turned around in his metal folding chair. "Ten bucks says they don't make the state line, Alicia."

I shot him the same dirty look I'd been sending his way since eighth grade. That's when he'd developed to his freakish size and decided it was his birthright to lord it over the rest of us who were actually normal. He was a football player and going on a scholarship to some backwater division-three school in Florida. That's not to say he wasn't smart. He was actually one of only five of us who'd opted to take AP physics during senior year. Win and I were also in there. Me because I was already thinking that the more AP credits I could score, the less my parents would have to shell out for tuition if I decided to go to college. Win because his parents made him.

But since there were only five of us, they couldn't actually give us a teacher, so Mr. Booker had us meet in the supply closet attached to his classroom for the entire year. He'd come in once or twice a week for a few minutes when he could get away from the class of regular kids he had at the same time, but we were mostly on our own. Win was way more intent on trying to get Dave to punch him, so any studying we did was punctuated by Win making comments about Dave's mom, or Dave's beloved Dodge pickup, or phony theorems about the density of Dave's skull after all those hits he'd taken on the football field. I admit it was pretty entertaining for a while, watching Win yank Dave's chain, but after we bombed a couple of practice tests, it became clear that Win's idea of fun was costing us a lot more than we expected. Most days when we should have been working, I was listening to Dave and Win tear into each other, wondering whom I should be rooting for. Sometimes I wished Dave would just break Win's jaw so we could do whatever problems we were supposed to be working on.

In the end none of us even signed up for the exam.

"We're going the whole distance, Dave," Win said coolly.

Dave snorted. "You don't have it in you. Don't have that killer instinct . . . the drive," he said, sounding eerily like the future physical-education teacher he was destined to become.

"How would you know?" I asked.

"'Cause guys like you just don't," he said.

Guys like us? What was that supposed to mean?

"And what are you doing this summer?" Win asked him.

Dave was quiet a moment. "Working," he said finally. Alicia was watching us all with interest.

"Working?" Win's voice sounded playful. "That sounds exciting—mature, even. And where will you be *working*?" he asked, stressing the last word, like the concept was completely alien to him. For a guy who'd never so much as taken out the trash, it sort of was.

Dave shifted back in his seat, pretended to listen to the vice principal's threats of Breathalyzers tomorrow night. "My grandparents' farm. Setting tobacco, mostly . . . it's good conditioning for football next fall," he added, but the swagger had gone out of his voice.

"Well," Win said, "good luck with that, Davey. I hope you find it very fulfilling. *Guys like us*, however"—he hooked a thumb at me—"well, we're just not cut out for that kind of summer."

But Dave retained a shred of that idiot obstinacy—the same quality that allowed him to think of football as the only real sport. "You'll never make it."

"I'll take that bet," Alicia said.

Something in the universe of high school life was shifting. Maybe Alicia was on our side only to make a buck. Maybe only because she was as bored with Dave's routine as the rest of us. Maybe she actually wanted us to make it. At any rate, it was a first.

"You won't be sorry," Win said as the band fired up again with the alma mater and we all rose for the mandatory sing-along.

CHAPTER FIVE

"Sorry, I couldn't call sooner, Mom, I left my phone in the room by mistake. Just got in."

"Christopher?" My mother sounded as panicked as I knew she would. My roommate appeared to be studying—though since classes didn't start until Monday, I couldn't be sure what.

"Yeah, it's me," I said.

"We got you that phone so we could stay in touch. It doesn't do anyone any good if we can't contact you," my mother said. My parents had broken down and added me to the cell phone plan before I left for school. I think Win's disappearance had Mom spooked, but Dad said it would just be cheaper than paying long-distance charges anyway. But I knew it was a sacrifice on top of so many more they'd made for me to be here.

"Sorry, Mom. I still can't get used to carrying it around."

She ignored me. "Christopher, an *FBI agent* called here this morning," she whispered.

"Mom, you're whispering."

"I am not," she continued in a slightly less hushed tone.

"Nobody's tapping the phone, Mom," I said. At least, I didn't think anyone was tapping the phone.

"Don't change the subject!"

I gave up. "Some guy named Ward just left."

"That's who called us! You already spoke with him?" she asked. "What did he say? Did he harass you?"

"Mom, it's cool. Just calm down," I said. "Is Dad there?" She often needed my father to talk her off the ledge.

"I'm on the extension, Chris," my dad said. "Just got home. Helluva day, too. Tried to set that sign at the new Applebee's on 64, but the wind was just—"

"Allen!" my mother shrieked. "Our son has been interrogated by the FBI! Our Win is missing! No one cares about the sign!"

"It was no big deal," I lied. "He just wanted to know about the trip, whose idea it was, if I'd heard from Win."

"Have you?" my mother asked.

"No," I admitted. "Since Coggans stopped calling last week, I sort of thought maybe that meant Win had come back."

"Lydia Coggans hasn't called me back in that long at least," my mother offered. She'd been calling daily to see if they'd heard from Win.

"How about the nonexistent uncle in Seattle?" my dad asked.

"Also news to me," I said.

"Why do you think they didn't ever ask you about that one in all those conversations we had after you got back?" he asked.

"Probably the same reason Mr. Coggans didn't give me a heads-up about sending an FBI agent my way."

"Oh, *Christopher*," my mother said. She only called me Christopher when she felt especially maternal or when I was in trouble. Now both applied. "Christopher, how could you not have known? How could he have lied about that?"

I sighed. "All I know is what I told you. What I just told the investigator. We've been through all this a hundred times." After I showed up without Win and my mom wigged out, we must have been over the events at least that often. Mom was beside herself, Dad was concerned, and we even sat down with Win's parents for only the second time in the history of our friendship.

"He believe you?" my father asked.

"I don't know. I sound pretty stupid. I guess I did overlook a few details."

"Just tell the truth, Chris," my dad said calmly. "It'll sort itself out."

"Of course he'll tell the truth, Allen," my mother snapped. "Our son is an honest boy. If he says he doesn't know what happened to Win, then I believe him." She sounded near tears. She sounded as if she was trying to convince herself. She *doubted* me.

"You're right, Nancy," my father said in the same tone I'd heard hostage negotiators use in movies.

"Oh," my mother cried, "I just hope Win's all right. But how could he be all right if he hasn't contacted his parents?" I wanted to point out that he'd apparently not spoken to them for the entirety of our trip and was as happy then as I'd ever seen him.

"Mom, can I talk to Dad for a second?" I asked.

"Chris, you know you can tell me anything," she said. But that wasn't entirely accurate. Like what I'd been doing in the bathroom all those times. Luckily, my father intervened.

"Nance, trust the boy. I'll fill you in. If he wants to talk to me, let him."

I could sense my mother forming replies in her mind. Even imagined her opening her mouth once or twice to frame the words. But instead of a protest, finally, she said, "Well . . ."

"I'll call you Monday, Mom," I said. "After the detective guy comes again."

"He's coming back?" she yelped. "We have to get you a lawyer, you don't have to talk to him—"

My father cut her off. "Honey, I'll just be a minute with Chris."

"Wouldn't you like me to call Mr. Shaw?" she asked.

"Nancy, he's a tax attorney," my father said evenly.

She hesitated again. "Well . . . fine," she said, adding, "I love you, Chris."

"Love you, too, Mom," I mumbled into the phone.

Mom's connection went quiet. My father and I were silent a second.

"You okay, son?" he asked.

"Think so. It's just . . . weird," I said.

More silence. Then my father took a deep breath, like he was about to dive underwater. "What happened out there, Chris?" he asked.

"Everything, Dad," I said. "Everything."

CHAPTER SIX

"Everything about high school is behind you boys," Winston Coggans the *Second* said proudly that night at dinner after graduation. Winston the *Third* and I had managed to get through the marching and ceremony without incident. It was this part I'd truly been dreading. My parents had invited Win and his family to join us for dinner. I don't think any of us were more surprised than Win that they accepted. But it was nothing compared with the shock Win's mom experienced after arriving at the restaurant Win and I had chosen—the same place we celebrated my birthday last summer.

"Are those peanut shells on the floor?" she asked as a waitress clad in a tiny tank top, huge belt buckle, and tight jeans showed us to our table. Roundup was one of those fake-saloon, Western places, complete with the swinging half doors on the bathroom stalls and the bucket of raw peanuts on the table to shell and eat while you waited for your food. They also had monster steaks. Win and I figured we'd be eating peanut butter and ramen noodles all summer, so milking our parents for a free slab of meat was the only real choice.

"You're not allergic, are you?" my mother asked her.

Win's mother made a face that sort of looked like she wished she were. "Not technically."

After we'd ordered, and Win's parents had ceased looking like they'd stumbled into some foreign country, we tried to talk a little over the too-loud country music they piped in to make sure we remembered we were in a honky-tonk meat palace.

"Winston here's heading to Dartmouth, you know," his father said again, nodding to his son but looking to my father. If I didn't know any better, I'd say he seemed proud. But I did know better. If he was proud, it was only of himself for pulling in the right favors and leaning on the right people to get Win's 3.2 GPA into the Ivies.

"His grandfather played football for the Big Green, you know," Win's father said. "I was supposed to play lacrosse, but I injured my knee right before my freshman year. I loved it there, though, just like my father said I would. Just like I'm sure Win will."

Win nodded, smiling weakly. He was even less excited about school than I was.

"Funny how we sort of turn into our fathers, don't you think, Collins?" he asked my dad, reaching for a peanut.

Dad shrugged. "Hard to say. Mine died when I was nine."

"Shame. But I bet you are like him. I'm just like mine. He was like his before him," he said, extracting the peanut carefully from the shell, brushing away the papery hull. He seemed lost to himself for a moment. A half smile played at the corners of his mouth, but his eyes projected something else. Regret, maybe? I couldn't be sure. I'd never seen him like this.

He tossed the peanut into the ashtray. "In fact, Win's the fourth generation of Coggans men to join the Ivy League," he said.

"Yeah, but I'm the first to need a life coach to do it," Win said. I laughed. In addition to open manipulation by his father, his mother had made Win's acceptance her priority project during the spring of our junior year. She hired someone to help Win out with the application, get him into some volunteer work, and essentially pad his résumé.

"Winston," his father growled. My parents looked awkwardly at each other and to me. We all knew the show Coggans was putting on, but Win wouldn't let it go. I willed Win to leave well enough alone. We were saved by an unlikely source.

Win's mother had spent the entire postgraduation hugfest on her cell with a travel agent. It rang again as we sat waiting for our salads. After a brief exchange she hung up and turned to us. "I'm finally getting back to Tuscany," she said, snapping shut her tiny silver phone and reaching for her water glass, from which she plucked the straw as if it were a hair or something.

I couldn't remember when the woman *wasn't* on vacation. Win had gone with her only a couple of times—once to Europe, that I remembered, and another time she made him go with her to Ecuador, where they delivered a bunch of books and stuff to this school her Women's League sponsored. When she was home, she took a weird interest in Win, dragging him along to various charitable organizations she chaired, fund-raising events that she threw her name and money behind. Win told me once that he sort of thought it was her way of spending quality time with him.

His dad was always too busy working to go with them anywhere, and when we hit ninth grade, she claimed she didn't feel right about pulling Win out of school. Most of the time she traveled with her sister. Mrs. Coggans never fit in West Virginia anyway.

"You must be very proud," I said to Win.

He nodded. "They grow up so fast, don't they?"

"Stop it, Winston," his mother said, almost playing along. "You know it's been a while. I just hope Cinque Terre hasn't become too overrun with those backpackers," she gushed, looking to my mother for sympathy.

"Either way you'll have a lot of stories to swap with the boys when everyone gets back," said my mother, who'd only been as far as Niagara Falls.

Win's mother looked confused, though whether it was mention of the bike trip or the prospect of conversation with her son, who could say?

"Oh! The bike trip! Right. I only wish they'd gone last summer. All that self-discovery and adventure and whatnot. Colleges eat that stuff up," she said to Mom, before turning to Win. "But we managed, didn't we, sweetie?" she said, reaching for Win's hand. "Still, I can't imagine how much smoother that interview might have gone if you'd had that to fall back on," she said, shaking her head lightly.

After a beat Mom tried again. "I don't know if I could have been talked into it last year, but I'm pretty excited for the boys now," she said. "Though I confess I'm more than a little nervous."

She'd been crying quietly off and on all afternoon and began dabbing her eyes with a napkin.

"They'll be fine, Nancy," my father said, reaching behind my mother and rubbing the nape of her neck, stroking the few hairs that had escaped the clip that held the rest of it up. With the other hand he loosened the tie she had made him wear for the occasion. "Adventure's good for a couple of young men." He gave us both a smile. "Don't you think this trip is a pretty good way to spend a summer, Coggans?"

For a moment I panicked. It struck me that if Win's parents actually talked long enough to my mom and dad, they'd all four figure out that no one had actually granted us permission.

"Oh," Win's father said, "I suppose it's all right." He turned to Win. "Just get it out of your system so you can come back and get serious about your life."

My parents didn't say anything, though my dad looked like he had just eaten a rotten peanut.

"Will do, Dad," Win said evenly. "Will do."

Win's mother's cell rang again, and within moments she was yelling at her travel agent. "What do you mean Air Italia only has coach tickets left for the Milan flight? Check the other airlines!"

The salads arrived and were set before us. I dumped the carafe of ranch dressing over mine and dove in, glad for a reason not to talk.

Win's father placed his napkin in his lap and reached for his fork. His mother said something into her phone and pulled it away for a moment. "She's got a ticket. For tomorrow afternoon. But that means I have to catch the early connection out of Charleston to make it. Can you drop me?" she said to her husband.

"What time? I tee off at nine," he said.

"You'll make it."

Then they looked at Win. "What time are you leaving?" his mother asked.

He looked quickly at me, then at my mom and dad. "Eight, probably." Win and I hadn't discussed our departure time at all. "I can just stay at Chris's tonight. My stuff's already there anyway."

"But you'll miss the big send-off," my mother said to his parents.

Mrs. Coggans pretended not to hear her. "You're sure you don't mind, Winston? This is really important to Mommy," she said, flashing a perfect smile. "If I grab this flight, your aunt Claire and I will have a whole extra day in Rome to recover before we sail for Capri."

"It's fine," Win said.

"But—" my mother began before Win cut her off.

"Really," he said, adding as he looked across the table at Mom, "no big deal."

Win's mother turned back to her phone and ordered the agent to buy the ticket. His father descended on his salad.

And that was the best Win might hope for in the emotional good-bye department. Their embraces of him in the parking lot after dinner seemed forced. Win's mother did look like she might tear up a bit as she held him, but then her phone rang again and she wandered away toward their car.

"See you soon," his father said, shaking his hand.

Win nodded. "Yeah. Soon."

His father held the grip a little longer, reaching out with his other hand and placing it on Win's shoulder. "You'll be careful. And you can call me if you need something," he said.

Win nodded. "Yeah."

"I meant what I said earlier, though," his father said, his tone hardening as he dropped his hand and stepped back.

"I know," Win said, sneaking a hand up to his face to wipe at his nose as his father turned away.

We all stood in the lot and watched them drive off. Finally my father shook his head and unlocked the car. "You guys need to get home and get some rest," he said. "Big day tomorrow." Win and I climbed in the backseat and got lost in the details of preparing to go.

At home my folks parked in the driveway and left us in the garage to finish our packing.

"Nice dinner, huh?" Win said finally.

"Painless enough, I guess," I said.

We busied ourselves with the careful packing of our panniers. The pile of stuff grew smaller as we found more ways to make it fit, checking each item off a list I'd made as we worked.

"Where's your sleeping bag?" I asked Win as I searched the floor of the garage.

Win took a look around. "Whoops."

I laughed. "You forgot your sleeping bag? That's pathetic," I said.

He shrugged. "Got an extra?"

I shook my head. "Only the one my dad used in the army. You don't want that one. We'll have to go pick yours up."

"Nah," he said. "Let's just go to the Super Wal-Mart. I'll buy one. It'll be faster."

"Win, it takes as long to drive to Huntington as it does to get to your house," I said.

"Just go ask your mom if we can borrow the car," he said.

After persuading Mom that we really were going to Wal-Mart instead of heading off to find an after-graduation kegger, she gave us the keys. We found ourselves back on the road, the moon high overhead as we shot down the driveway and headed up the hill toward town.

"Seriously, Win," I said. "Your house is closer."

"I don't want to go back to my house," he said deliberately. I couldn't say I blamed him. We curved around past a cluster of mobile homes topped by satellite dishes, each with a chained-up dog or aboveground pool in the yard.

We took I-64 into Huntington and pulled into the parking lot, where a few cars and faces I recognized from school were already cruising the loop from the Sno-Cone Hut to the turnaround here at the Supercenter. We found a spot close to the door and passed into the buzzing glare of twenty-four-hour fluorescent lights.

Win bought the lightest-weight bag we could find, and we were back in the car and headed for the freeway by eleven forty-five.

"Let's take the old highway back," Win said.

"Dude, we need to get back and crash. You're the one who decided we're leaving at eight tomorrow," I said.

"Just do it," he said.

I sighed and turned on my blinker, easing around the back of the strip mall to where the highway lay, forgotten. "Whatever."

The warm night air whipped through the open windows as we sped down the empty road. We passed the ball fields where Win and I had played Little League the three summers my dad coached our team. We passed the fancy neighborhood Win's family had moved from after somebody built a newer crop of minimansions closer to Hurricane. We passed the high school, the lights above the stadium now dark, though the outline of the tent on the football field was still visible in the moonlight.

"Pull in here," Win ordered as we reached the turnoff for the city park. I did. The lot was empty and quiet, the smell of chlorine heavy in the humid air.

"How many hours do you think we spent here?" Win said.

"Most of every summer," I admitted. Win and I had spent a few days a week here, swimming in the tiny public pool, staring at hot lifeguards as we got older, and eating greasy cheeseburgers from the concession stand.

"Is that the gazebo you built?" he asked, pointing toward the picnic shelter I'd built near the playground as my Eagle project.

"Yeah," I said.

He smiled. "After your house, I'll miss this place most."

"Why are you acting like you're shipping out with the foreign legion? We'll be back in two months, tops."

He didn't respond immediately, just kind of waved his arm around outside the window, feeling the air, the place. "Yeah," he said. "We'd better get some sleep."

Neither of us slept much. I was too keyed up, and Win kept dredging up dumb old stories from the pool or elementary school. But we stumbled into the kitchen the next morning at seven, ate the pancakes Mom made, and geared up. Even though I should have felt wiped, I was buzzing with excitement that we were finally leaving.

In our driveway Win turned to me. "Ready to get this out of your system?" The imitation of his father was too accurate to be funny.

My parents hugged us both, with Mom crying enough for two

sets of parents. That didn't surprise me. Win was as close to a second son as she'd ever get, and I'd heard her mutter more than once what she'd do with him if he were hers to raise. Plus, Mom cried at everything. Mormon commercials, makeover shows, birthday cards.

What shocked me was that Win had tears in his eyes as well.

Win and I approached our bikes. He looked at his appraisingly. "Let's see what this old pony can do!" He threw a leg over the top tube and mounted up.

I hugged my mom again, gave my dad a nod, and hopped onto my bike. Win was waiting on me, riding his brakes so he barely inched forward on the downhill. A second later we were rolling down the driveway side by side.

"Did you pack the sandwiches I made you?" Mom shouted down as we neared the road.

I looked back at her, my helmet blocking part of my vision. I could see only her arm, held out to us as we slipped away from her. "Got 'em, Mom. Thanks."

"Watch out for roadkill, travelers," my dad shouted.

"And we'll try to avoid becoming roadkill," I joked. My mom immediately started crying harder.

"I hear sun-dried possum is quite the delicacy," Win said.

We reached the bottom of the driveway and tapped the hand brakes lightly. The bikes, each loaded with about forty pounds' worth of gear, took a little longer to slow on the incline.

"Make sure you look both ways," Win said. "Your mommy's still watching."

I laughed, released the brakes, and cranked hard on my pedal, merging onto the sycamore-lined road.

CHAPTER SEVEN

The sub I'd wolfed down in the commons sat heavy in my stomach as I raced across campus to my one o'clock: English 102. I ducked into the computer lab on the first floor of Skiles Hall. That morning I'd already endured a chemistry class and a physics lecture, both professors apparently intent on scaring the crap out of us. But I was glad for the distraction. It saved me from replaying the conversations with Ward and my folks in my head like I had been doing all weekend. Obsessing about these discussions inevitably led to me obsessively worrying about Win. Ward's suggestion that something had happened to him sent my mind through all sorts of scenarios. It wasn't likely Win had been hit by a truck or anything. Somebody would have called. Win had his driver's license on him, and if he'd been hit it would have been just a matter of time before they found his ID. But it also didn't make sense that he hadn't contacted home. Or at least me. Somewhere in my mind a voice told me that Win would have called me at least. It wasn't necessarily Win's nature to think about the other guy, but at some point I figured he'd realize that he'd probably left a bit of a mess back here and would at least let me know he was okay.

But any logic I tried to project onto Win seemed to bounce right off him. And when I thought back to the final moments of our ride together on that pass in the Cascades, nothing made sense. I could easily imagine him tangled up with his bike at the bottom of one of those steep curves we rode. I could imagine him ending up there by accident, or even on purpose. The latter possibility freaked me out most of all. I'm sure people with less to worry about had done themselves in. But I could also picture him riding south down the Washington coast, a beach to his right and a crosswind trying to push him into traffic.

Still, I held out some hope that he'd contact me, which was why I'd been obsessively checking my e-mail since Ward left on Thursday afternoon. If I knew Win like I thought I did, he'd probably duck into a public library and send off some smart-ass message. And when I thought of that, and the fact that he was probably out there having fun while I dealt with this mess and the life I was supposed to be living, it really started to piss me off.

I'd been alternating between bouts of fear and rage like this. And everybody kept telling me how much fun I was going to have in college, how much freedom I'd have. I was starting to believe that I'd used up my lifetime quota of both on the trip this summer. Starting to wonder if I was too young to get an ulcer.

I signed on quickly to the network, using the new user name and password I'd been issued during orientation. I bypassed the new school account they'd given me and went straight to my old e-mail. But there was nothing new waiting in my in-box since I checked it last night. Just to be thorough, I returned to the Georgia Tech home page, clicked the student mail account link, and entered my user name and password again. I scrolled quickly through the junk the university sent out—past the reminder about the extra days off around Labor Day coming up, past the notice that the fitness center pool hours had changed, past an invitation to a meeting from the Outdoor Club, whose information sheet I'd signed during orientation last week. The fourth message made me sit up a little taller. I clicked on the sender's name: wcoggans.

Win had figured out my e-mail address at school? Maybe he was sending it to this account because he figured the other one was, what, being monitored?

But when I opened the e-mail and saw the full address, the weight that seemed to have lifted just slightly at the hope of having heard from Win, of having some proof that he was alive, and maybe even something I could hand over to the FBI guy so he could find him and stop bothering me, descended to my stomach and threatened to displace that sandwich.

The message was from wcoggans@titanchem.com.

Great.

Win's *father* had my address. Probably an easy bit of information for him to pick up, given his resources, but I hadn't even bothered to give it to my mom yet. The message was brief.

> I urge you to extend your full cooperation
>
> to my associate Mr. Ward. In spite of recent
>
> inconsistencies, I've always maintained that you
>
> are an honorable young man. I've every reason to
>
> believe you want this scenario to draw quietly
>
> to its conclusion, as I do. If not, I can certainly
>
> help you to find additional motivation.

That was it. No greeting. No signature. No apology for springing an FBI agent on me during my first week of college. No demonstration of concern for Win.

It was this that surprised me least.

Automatically I hit the reply button and placed my fingers on the keyboard. But then I stopped. I never knew what to say to Mr. Coggans, and that certainly hadn't changed now. I'd deal with this later.

I logged out, jumped up from the machine, and bolted from the room and up the stairs to room 214.

"Welcome to a brand-new state of mind," Dr. Flynn Lenoir said from the front of the classroom as I walked in and took the last empty seat in the second row. "Welcome to an odyssey of literature, truth, and the human spirit." He beamed at us, bushy black hair sticking out at odd angles. He popped his smudged glasses back up to the bridge of a round nose.

A few seats over a kid raised a tentative hand. "Is this English Lit 102?"

"Some may call it that," he said, "but I prefer to think of it as my mission field." He leaned forward on the lectern. "Tech is a fine institution, and you should all count yourselves lucky to be here. But over the past twelve years"—he paused to look around the room, studying faces that I'm pretty sure were as bewildered as mine—"I've come to realize that we've a dangerous tendency in higher education, particularly at schools as specialized as this one, to turn out . . . well . . . somewhat one-sided individuals."

If I didn't know any better, I'd be pretty sure this guy was angling to piss off the math-science nerd contingent. Even though technically I was one of them, I liked his style already. After my first two classes it was sort of refreshing.

"So I've made it my life's work to lead the science-minded down the path of true enlightenment. This course is not just a hoop you must jump through in order to get back to your 'real' coursework. This course is absolutely, vitally necessary. For if the best scientific minds in the world have no sense of beauty, art, purpose, or truth, then we are all lost," he boomed.

I glanced around the room. Half my classmates looked as clueless as I felt. The other half were already flipping madly through the course bulletin, searching for other sections of English they could switch to.

"But," he shouted, "before we can delve into the mysteries of human nature and universal truth, we must know who our fellow travelers are."

He acted as if we were supposed to know what that meant. After too long a pause for a school with a supposed entrance requirement of a combined ACT score of 29, a girl in the front row hazarded a translation.

"You want us to introduce ourselves?"

"No, my dear, I want you to introduce one another. Please find a partner. You will have ten minutes to get to know each other, asking as many questions as possible. At the end of that time you will be asked to deliver a brief introduction. Over the course of the next two classes—while the less adventurous in our midst fall away from the pursuit of truth in favor of safer English courses—we'll get to know one another."

He paused and looked around the room at the students poring over the class schedule. He rolled his eyes. "Questions?"

There were a million I could think of: *Why are we doing this? Where's the syllabus? How'd you end up with a name like Flynn Lenoir?* But nobody said a word.

"Then, please make a new acquaintance," he said, and left the room.

There were a few beats of silence, but then the place erupted.

"This guy's nuts."

"I've heard he's really good."

"Is he allowed to just leave us in here like this?"

"Did you check out that tie?"

"Anybody know if Technical Writing is full? I've heard that's easy."

Eventually a handful of folks began settling down, digging out notebooks, and finding partners. I realized that on this day, the first of my college career, I was acutely aware of Win's absence. The concern and anger I'd had for him since I learned he was AWOL were now replaced by something else. Panic. Win had been my partner in stuff like this for the last decade.

"Got a partner yet?" a girl in front of me asked. I tried to speak but couldn't. There were no girls like this back in Hurricane. Girls at home had dirty-brown hair or fake blond. Nothing like the long black hair this girl had pulled into a loose ponytail. Girls at home wore makeup like war paint, their faces always a shade or two darker than their necks. But this girl didn't seem to have a trace of anything on her face, and her skin—arms, neck, all of it that I could see without overtly checking her out—glowed with the same even brown. And you'd never find eyes that deep back home. Never.

The only word to describe her was "exotic." Only not in the dancing-on-a-pole sense. The other kind.

I shook my head. Maybe not having Win as my partner was a very good thing.

She stared at me. "Well?"

I *really* wanted to say the right thing. "Huh?"

She rolled her eyes and smiled. "Do you want to be my partner?"

Yes, please. "Sure."

She turned her desk around to face mine. "I'm Vanti," she said.

"Chris. What kind of name is Vanti?" Idiot! I tried again. "I mean . . . it's so unusual," I stumbled.

"It's actually short for Avantika. It means 'princess of some place or other.' I was born in Punjab." When I didn't register the reference, she added, "In India."

"Chris, skinny white kid from West Virginia," I said. "But I've no idea what my name means."

"Nice to meet you, Chris." She laughed.

"Likewise."

"What do you think of Lenoir?" she asked, reaching for a pen.

I shrugged. "I think I'll stick it out. Seems entertaining at least."

She nodded. "I'm staying too."

I grabbed my pencil and began to write. "'Princess Vanti of Punjab.' What else should I say when I introduce you?"

She sighed and looked up at the ceiling, stuck the end of her pen in her mouth. I was in love. "I don't know. I'm from DC . . . forward on the soccer team . . . I like dogs," she said.

I nodded as I wrote. "Good start. Major?"

"Premed, I think," she said. "I'll let you know."

"You like Atlanta?" I asked.

"Other than the fact that you can't find decent Indian food it's okay."

"Well, you can't find anything decent on campus, period," I said.

"True. But I did find some killer Mexican food. I got here two weeks ago for soccer tryouts. After Saturday practices the captains take us to this little place with awesome guacamole. The veterans love it because they don't card and will give anybody a margarita, but not me. My dad would totally deport me, and he *would* find out. But the flautas! Oh, man. I'll just have to take you sometime so you can understand."

I was on a campus where the male-female ratio was two to one. I'd managed to connect with surely the most beautiful freshman and she'd just asked me out.

"Sorry," she said, suddenly embarrassed. "I didn't mean that the way it sounded."

Okay. Accidentally asked out. But still.

"So anyway," she said, blushing. "What about you? I've told you a lot about me and managed to humiliate myself. Your turn."

"Embarrassing myself is sort of a hobby. Fire away."

"I should write that down," she said, smiling into her notebook.

"Don't worry. I'll probably end up giving a demonstration."

"Family?" she asked.

"Also embarrassing," I said.

"No. I mean tell me about your family."

"One mom, one dad," I said.

"Major?"

"Aeronautical engineering—I guess."

She jotted and nodded.

"Sports?"

"Biking, mainly. That's what I did all summer, at least."

She looked up from her notes. "Racing or something?"

I shook my head. "No. My friend Win and I rode our bikes out to the Pacific Northwest."

She stared at me a second. "Like . . . bikes you pedal?"

This was a moment I loved. I'd loved it all the way across the country when people found out how far we'd come under just our own power. The trick here was to avoid playing it too big and thereby letting the other person know how much I loved the look of surprise, then the unguarded admiration.

I just nodded.

"No motors? No ridiculous wearing of black leather?"

I laughed. "No. There was some spandex I'd rather not discuss, though."

"Wow," she said, putting down her pen. "That's really amazing."

For the next eight minutes she wanted to know how long it had taken, what all we'd seen, how we'd gotten the idea. By the time

Dr. Flynn Lenoir re-entered the classroom, we were laughing at something I'd said and she was smiling this really warm smile that made me sort of dig college in a way I hadn't yet.

Lenoir looked at his wrist and announced we had just enough time for one brave pair to start things off. He wasn't actually wearing a watch.

"Would anyone like to go first?"

Before I could say anything, Vanti had her hand in the air. "Chris and I will."

I started to protest, but she stood, turned, and flashed a smile that would have made me crawl across broken glass if she'd asked. I ripped out the page where I'd taken my notes and joined her at the front of the room.

"You go first," she whispered. "I'll seem totally boring if you introduce me after I've talked about your adventures."

"No way you could ever be boring," I said back, maybe a bit louder than I meant to, because Flynn Lenoir gave this heavy moan and smiled goofily from his seat next to the podium.

Then I blushed. "See?" I said to Vanti. "Told you I'd end up demonstrating."

To avoid further embarrassment, I dove in, covering her short bio and love for Mexican food in less than a couple of minutes. The part of the class that wasn't still looking for a new course to join applauded weakly as I concluded. Then it was her turn.

"This is Chris Collins from Hurricane, West Virginia. He rode his *bike* across the country this summer," she gushed. I didn't hear the rest. Didn't hear her mention my family or retell one of the funny stories. I heard only one thing—Chris, *not* Chrisandwin.

CHAPTER EIGHT

"You want to stop?" Win asked me as we crested a hill somewhere in the third hour of our post-lunch ride. We'd covered almost thirty miles that morning before we broke to eat at a city park in Leon.

"No, I'm good," I said.

We'd been having the exact same exchange for the last ten miles. I was pretty sure we both would have been happy to call it a day at the last campground we passed, but every time one of us asked the other, it was like some weird, dumb challenge not to be the one to go weak first.

"Yeah, I'm good too," Win said. We rode quietly for a few minutes before Win spoke again.

"Dude, my butt hurts," he complained, signaling an end to our standoff.

"Yeah, the padding isn't quite getting it done," I said, referring to the half inch of gel cushioning sewn into the lining of my bike shorts. I stood on my pedals to let some blood move back into that spot.

"I'm pretty sure," Win huffed as he topped out just behind me, "that all this pressure and heat on my boys might make me sterile."

"Bonus. No way should you be allowed to reproduce," I shouted over my shoulder as we picked up speed on a downhill. In the distance I could see the Ohio River bridge and the state line, maybe a five-minute ride away.

"Car back," Win yelled, and I sidled more toward the shoulder of the road in an automated response. The car roared past, kicking up too much exhaust, the radio blaring "Sweet Home Alabama" just a little too loud.

"I'll be glad to get to a place where Lynyrd Skynyrd isn't considered refined musical craftsmanship," Win said.

"Almost there," I said. "Ohio, dead ahead."

"Right," Win said. "Ohio's just like West Virginia only without the hillbilly jokes."

A hundred yards from the bridge I pulled to a stop next to a sign declaring LEAVING WEST VIRGINIA. Win pulled up beside me.

"Like it's a warning or something," he said, shaking his head.

I laughed. "Let's take a picture."

Win rolled his eyes. "Promise me that you won't be taking pictures of every mile marker in Iowa."

"This is a big deal," I reasoned. "We've never ridden out of state before."

Still, Win unclipped his other pedal and swung his leg over the bike.

"Gimme your camera," I said. Win had a digital. I had a pair of disposable point-and-shoots to last me the whole trip.

He sighed but obeyed, rummaging for the camera in his handlebar bag. "You sound like those damn Hobbits," he said. "'Take one more step and it will be the farthest I've ever been from the Shire. . . .'"

"I'm not the one who memorized all three *Lord of the Rings* movies. That was you, remember?" I snatched the camera from his hand.

"Tricksey Hobbitses stole my precious!" he hissed, lunging for the Nikon with his free hand as I slid it from the neoprene case.

"Just go stand by the sign," I ordered, dodging his reach. Win relented, leaned his bike against mine in a sort of tepee, and walked over to the sign.

My handlebar bag had a flat, clear lid for holding the map, and it made a perfect shelf for balancing the camera. I arranged the shot and hit the timer.

"Helmets on or off?" I asked as I trotted over.

"Uh, off," Win muttered as he clawed at the catch. The timer was beeping steadily as I reached him and unclipped my own helmet, running my fingertips through my matted hair.

As the light flashed on the camera front and the beep sped up, Win and I stood next to each other, helmets tucked under our arms like a couple of astronauts in a NASA promotional photo. Neither of us smiled. The beeping climaxed with an understated click.

"Well, there's the album cover," Win said. "Now let's find a place to crash in the Buckeye State."

I returned to my bike, chucked the camera and case at Win, and studied the map. "According to this, there's a campground just over the line," I said.

"Good. I'm hungry. And did I mention the boys are in trouble?"

Twenty minutes later we reached our destination: the Rest-a-While Campground.

"What kind of campground is this?" Win said.

I shrugged. It didn't look like I'd imagined, based on the few state or national parks my family had camped in during summer vacations. A narrow ribbon of patchy asphalt split a strip of grass that cut back between the fields on either side. At the far end sat a small, run-down house. In two rows on either side of the house a half dozen RVs sat parked, each plugged into its own outlet for water and electricity.

"See any tents?" I asked as we rolled up.

"No," Win said as a man emerged from the house at the end. "But that guy can probably tell us where to set up."

The man was wearing a pair of denim overalls covered in drops and smears of what appeared to be the entire color history of the little shack. He had no shirt on beneath the bib, but around his waist he wore a tool belt stocked with a random assortment of gear, including a walkie-talkie, a couple of screwdrivers, and a ring of keys. He stood at the bottom of a short flight of steps, eyeing us cautiously from a safe twenty feet away.

"What do you want?" the guy said from beneath a ball cap advertising motor oil.

"How much for tent sites?" I asked.

He didn't respond as he reached behind him and pulled a flashlight from one of the pockets of his tool belt. He turned it on and pointed it at us, shining it straight into my eyes and then Win's before scanning the bikes.

It was only six o'clock and there was plenty of light left.

"No tent sites," the man said, still shining his light at Win's front pannier. "We're not set up for that."

"But this is a campground, right?" I said. "The map has a little green tent on it right here." I pointed gently at the map, my fingertip resting on the small green icon denoting a campground just outside Hanersville, Ohio. "I guess we'll pay the RV price. . . ."

"RV sites is twelve dollars, but we ain't set up for *those*," he said, gesturing again at the bikes with his flashlight, which I now noticed was pink.

"Well, we're not going to use power or anything, and really all we need is a place to set up our tent, if we could get some water from the hose or whatever," I said hopefully.

He shook his head. "The lady wouldn't like that."

I shot Win a look. He was staring at the flashlight, the beginnings of a smile starting at his mouth.

"The lady?" I said.

"Lady owns this campground. My wife. She wouldn't like this," he said. "Not civil."

I looked around at the RVs, piles of empty pop cans strewn like landscaping across the makeshift yards.

"I don't understand—," I began.

"Isn't that a kids' flashlight?" Win asked, pointing at the pink plastic light the man clutched.

He ignored Win. "The lady wouldn't like it," he repeated. "You'll mess on the grass."

The piles of junk and the oil leaking from the undersides of the RVs had surely done plenty of damage already.

"Seriously, my little cousin in New Jersey has a light just like that. Only hers has this little thing you can put on the front that makes the light change from purple to pink to yellow. . . ." Win leaned a little closer. "Looks like yours broke off."

The man stood up straighter and held the light like he might try to prove to us that in spite of its girly origins, it could still inflict some pain.

"Shut up, Win," I said. "Sir, I promise you we won't mess up the grass. The tent isn't very big—"

"He thinks we're going to poop in his yard, Chris," Win said, starting to laugh. "He didn't say 'mess *up* the grass,' he said 'mess *on* the grass.'" Then Win collapsed across his handlebars, shoulders convulsing with laughter.

"The lady wouldn't like that!" the man said louder, holding the light a little higher this time.

"Um, okay," I said, edging my bike backward. "Well, do you know where we might be able to camp instead?"

Win sat up straight and stopped laughing. "Yeah, maybe someplace they're not totally psycho?"

It took a half second for the man to realize that he—and by extension, his lady—had been insulted. I swore at Win, turned my wheel, and started to ride. Win just stood there laughing a second longer before he joined me. The man was walking toward us now. "Time to go," Win said.

"The lady wouldn't like this!" the man shouted as we rode away.

Win shouted over his shoulder, across the forty feet of black-top that now separated us. "Well, I'm pretty sure we wouldn't like the lady. Tell her the yard isn't even worth taking a dump in!" he said as the little pink flashlight sailed dangerously close to his ear, clattered to the pavement, and began rolling toward the road.

"Holy crap!" I said.

Win laughed louder as we pulled away. I shifted up a gear for good measure and looked back to check on Win's position, only to find him slowing at the bottom of the driveway, where he stopped, quickly reached down to retrieve the fallen flashlight, and then clipped back into his pedal as the man drew closer.

"Win, come on!"

He began to pedal, leaving the campground behind as he pulled even with me.

"Least we're not leaving empty-handed," he said, waving the flashlight at me.

"Great. We can use it to light up the road while we ride in the dark looking for a place to sleep," I muttered.

"We'll find something," he said.

"In another twelve miles." I spat, pulling away a bit.

"In time I think you'll come to recognize the hilarity of the situation," Win said.

I didn't respond, but I knew it was funny. And if I hadn't been tired and hungry and sore as hell, I would probably have been laughing with him. But we needed a place to sleep.

Five miles later Win spoke again. "Light's fading."

"Seven miles to go," I said. "Keep pedaling."

"Or we could scamp," he said.

"Excuse me?"

"Scamp. You know . . . sneak around, scam a free campsite . . ."

As pissed as I was at him, I didn't want to ride any farther. "Ah, *scamping*."

We stopped and looked around. A sign for an Assemblies of God church about twenty yards ahead was all we could see in either direction. There was a stand of thick pines, and we could hear water falling somewhere nearby.

"Scamping it is," I said as we pushed our bikes off the road and headed into the trees.

A few minutes later we'd found our home for the night.

"Nice spot," I said, tossing my helmet to the ground in a small clearing a hundred yards from the road. It was. A narrow stream ran nearby where we could filter water to cook the mac and cheese we'd stolen from Mom's stash. Best of all, it was in the only place guaranteed not to see any action on a Saturday night: the grounds of an isolated country church. It felt good—vaguely dangerous—to be getting away with something.

"The lady would approve," he said, adding, "And the price is right."

"Where's the aspirin?" I asked as I pulled the tent and ground sheet off my rear rack.

He shrugged, removing his shoes. "How should I know,

Eagle?" he asked, peeling off a pair of socks that I could smell from ten feet away. "You packed."

I threw the tent onto the carpet of brown needles. "But you were supposed to pack the first-aid kit, dork," I said. "Didn't you get any aspirin?"

"Just Band-Aids . . . toenail clippers . . . the essentials," he said.

"Toenail clippers? Since when are toenail clippers essential?"

"Since I get blisters on my toes if my nails get too long," he said as if I were the one testing his patience. "I didn't bring any aspirin, but I'd be happy to offer you a pedicure later. It's quite soothing."

I said nothing, merely tugged the tent out of the bag and unrolled it with a snap.

"So, no on the pedicure, then?"

As penance Win limped over to help me set up the tent without even being asked. We snapped the poles into place and threaded them through the guides attached to the fabric and had it up and open to the air in a matter of minutes. I was moving slowly, amazed by the soreness in my tailbone, and Win was already yawning.

We stripped the panniers off the bikes and stowed them inside the tent with our unrolled sleeping bags and pads. Win dug the stove and the food bag out. I snatched up the filter and went to fill our water bottles. It was quiet, save for the sputtering roar of the WhisperLite stove, the aluminum pot rattling away on the flame. I was pumping away at the filter, one tube floating in the halfhearted current of the stream for the intake, the other end running into my bottle. I could get used to this.

But then the unthinkable happened. A car turned off the main road (we could hear it more than actually see it) and onto the gravel pathway leading up to the church. The driveway was closer to our spot — so close that I could see the driver was wearing a yellow tie and had too much hair spray in his hair. Through the open window the breeze flapped at the edge of his lapel, but his hair stayed stiff, looking like a bike helmet.

"Don't move," I heard Win whispered.

"It's not a *T. rex*, dude," I said, harkening back to a shared fifth-grade obsession with *Jurassic Park*. "Besides, the tree cover is pretty heavy. He won't see us."

"He probably works here. Just came to pick . . ."

Win stopped short as another car turned off the highway and sidled down the same gravel road. It pulled neatly in line with the first, and a woman emerged bearing a casserole dish covered in foil.

"Think she works here too?" I asked.

Three more cars caravanned into the lot. The third had a backseat full of kids, one of whom was staring out the window at our spot. He immediately began shouting and pointing in our direction.

"Damn," Win muttered. "So much for the perfect campsite." I nodded, moved toward the bikes, and shoved the bottles back into the cages bolted to the tubes.

"You stuff the sleeping bags," I said to Win, "I'll get the tent."

"What are they doing here on a Friday night?" Win asked as he slipped into his shoes. "They must be some kind of super-Christians or something." Two of the men were approaching our site through the woods now. Neither Win nor I come from particularly religious families. My father describes us as CEOs ("Christmas and Easter only"), but he says grace when the thought strikes him and I am not totally averse to praying myself. Win's father—who is actually a CEO—despises anything he doesn't do himself, and openly decries religion as something for the weak.

"Does that mean they're the nice kind, or the ones who'll pelt us with Bibles as we clear out?" I whispered as the helmet-haired man and another in jeans and a T-shirt reading GOD'S GYM entered the clearing.

"Evening, boys," the suited man said. "Nice night for a camp-out?"

"Yes, sir," I said. "Look, we're really sorry, we just thought it wouldn't be a big deal, and we couldn't find a campground, and . . . we'll move. Just give us a few minutes."

I began to pack up but was startled by his response. He laughed. "Move? Don't do that. We're glad to have you. Long as you clean up in the morning."

I was stunned. "Really?"

"Why not? Don't reckon anybody else is sleeping here tonight. Where you fellas heading?"

"Seattle, sir. We just left West Virginia this morning," I offered.

"Well, we're glad the Lord brought you our way," he said. His companion nodded in a way that made me a little uncomfortable, as if the whole thing were some kind of stupid destiny.

"Listen, boys. We don't usually have church on Saturday night—it being reserved for the sinning and all," he said, laughing, "but we're at the end of a revival. Got a potluck supper. Lot of good food. Pies."

He let the lure of pies sink in. Shrewd.

"Would you like to join us?" he asked.

I responded out of habit. Out of politeness. Possibly out of something that didn't want to go to this church with the nice people. "We couldn't impose—"

But Win, who hadn't said a word until now, piped in. "We'd love to."

And strangely enough, he sounded like he meant it.

A couple of hours later my stomach was stretched tight. I'd eaten third helpings of almost everything—including that weird Jell-O salad with the marshmallows, four pieces of fried chicken, and half a key lime pie. Between mouthfuls we'd answered a lot of questions about why we'd decided to ride our bikes to the West Coast and whether or not we'd been baptized. It was the last question that had made me favor the dine-and-dash. But they were only asking out of curiosity, in the same sort of tone that you might ask someone if they'd ever had sushi or broken a bone.

So we ended up in the sanctuary. I was so tired that everything seemed louder—the music, the lively preacher who'd been dancing around the little stage area for nearly an hour, the three hundred or so people amening on cue from the packed pews and folding chairs that had been brought to fill in spaces around the aisles. I was on overload.

"Jacob's name meant 'deceiver'! And let me tell you people, he'd done some deceiving in his day," hollered the preacher, wearing a bolo tie, from the altar. "He stole the birthright of his brother, ran away, got deceived himself. But did he learn?

No! He just went on out and fooled some more people."

He paused and let the weight of Jacob's sins sink in on us. "And do you know what he wanted then?"

"Tell us, Pastor!" shouted someone from the back.

"He wanted to go home! He wanted forgiveness. But did the Lord just let him waltz back and get it?"

"No, sir!" another voice shouted.

"No, sir, indeed!" the preacher shouted as he stalked back and forth on the carpeted platform. "Jacob had to wrestle with that angel, had to wrestle with his God," he spat. "And he was changed!"

Win slouched next to me. I knew I would fall instantly asleep if the room would only quiet down for a second. But that had more to do with the miles we'd covered and my full belly. The story was actually pretty interesting.

What I'd managed to piece together was that it was about Jacob, who'd done a lot of bad stuff in his life, and then wanted to go back and make up for it. Then God sent an angel down to wrestle with him. Only Jacob was strong and wouldn't let go. They fought all night; all the while Jacob said he wouldn't let go until he'd received a blessing. So the angel did it, but not before he'd jacked Jacob's hip all out of place and they'd trampled the entire field down to nothing.

An organ began to play. "Some of you are wrestling with the Lord *right now*," the preacher intoned. "And this moment—this very minute—he wants to bless you. It's time to get changed," he concluded as an organ and a piano on either side of the church fired up. The congregation began a marathon version of "Just as I Am"—the only hymn I knew by heart from our biannual visits to church.

I stood, swaying on my feet, drunk with saturated fat and exhaustion. A legion of people poured forward to the altar, some fell to their knees and wept on the carpeted steps. Some started waving their hands in the air and babbling words that I'm pretty sure weren't even an attempt at singing along.

"Dude. This is starting to freak me out a little," I whispered, before I realized I was talking to a skinny woman wearing a straw hat.

Win was gone.

I caught sight of him as he walked calmly toward the preacher. Win stepped to his side as the pastor cast an arm around his shoulder. They whispered something to each other. And then they appeared to be praying. Both had bowed heads, closed eyes. The preacher's lips moved furiously; Win nodded his head slightly at irregular intervals.

What was going on?

Then both heads rose, another short exchange, they shook hands, and Win headed back toward me. I stared at him as he wove his way through the mass of people waiting to weep at the altar or talk to the preacher. He returned my gaze as he came back to his spot at my side.

"What?" he asked, feigning innocence.

"What do you mean 'what'?" I said, sounding more alarmed than I meant to. "What were you doing up there?"

He shrugged. Smiled. "Just talking."

CHAPTER NINE

Monday after classes I headed to the
campus fitness center. It sucked to do my workout inside after two
months of glorious, daylong rides outdoors, but I still hadn't fixed
my chain and didn't have the time it would take to get far enough out
of Atlanta to actually enjoy any scenery. The alternative? My road
bike remained in my room, hanging on the wall, while I endured a
stationary bike and chem book for company. It also seemed like the
best way to avoid being in my room, where Ward could find me.

I'd also been trying to conjure some bike trip magic, hoping
Vanti might show up and see me looking simultaneously cool and
academic. But it wasn't working, and my legs were only cramping,
not itching even a little.

Halfway through a programmed hill workout and the chapter

I'd been assigned, I heard a voice that I hadn't been hoping to hear. "This seat taken?"

Abe Ward popped himself onto the stationary bike next to mine, ignoring the OUT OF ORDER sign and settling in. He wasn't dressed in workout clothes, just another version of the same getup from the other day.

"Oh," I said without breaking pace. "Hi."

"Didn't we have an appointment today, Chris?"

I closed my book and dropped it to the carpet beside my water bottle. "I sort of forgot," I lied. "How'd you find me?"

He smiled. "I'm an investigator, Chris, remember? It's my business to know people. To get inside their heads and figure out what they're thinking . . . what motivates them . . . plus, your roommate said you'd be here."

"Win's dad never settled for less than the best," I said, smiling in spite of everything. He wasn't pedaling, but he looked like he fit on the bike all the same. Probably a decent hill climber.

"So," he said, fiddling with the buttons on the console.

"I told you everything I knew the other day when you were here," I said.

He nodded, pushed the pedals of the bike in half a rotation. "Thought you might have remembered something over the weekend."

I reached up and punched a button, increasing the resistance on the machine. "Nope."

He looked around the workout room. "So let's just talk about Win, then," he said. "Was there anything weird in his behavior during the trip? Or maybe before you left?"

"Win's behavior was clinically weird, Agent Ward," I said.

"Call me Abe," he offered. "Go on."

"I mean, Win was always weird. Always said the wrong thing even when he knew it was the wrong thing. Nearly got himself punched every day of high school."

He smiled. "I think I'd like Win."

"Maybe. He's an acquired taste," I said. "Honestly, if we hadn't become friends so early, I'm not sure I would have been able to put up with him. He has a knack for pushing people's buttons. Especially his parents'."

Ward raised an eyebrow at this. "Doesn't every eighteen-year-old?"

I let the generalization slide. "Not like Win. I remember in third grade he won the school spelling bee. In the final round it was down to two kids—him and this sixth grader. They both missed a word, so neither was out. After the sixth-grade kid missed another word that Win got right, he won. But when he told his dad the story that night, Coggans didn't congratulate him. Just asked him why he'd misspelled 'onyx.'"

Ward dropped his chin, gave a shift of his shoulders.

"After that it seemed like all Win knew he could do was disappoint them, so he made an art of it."

"What about before or during the trip? Any changes then?" he asked.

Too many to count. Instead I said, "Not really. Well, yeah. It's kind of hard to explain to someone who hasn't been there, but doing something like that changes you."

"Any signs of instability?" he asked.

"No more than usual," I said honestly.

"Anything that made you suspicious?" he asked.

The questions were like riding a stationary bike—lots of spinning the wheels, but no movement. "I'm trying to get through my first week of college. I've told you everything I know. Do you think I did something to Win or not?"

He stared at me, measuring his response. Finally he spoke. "No, Chris. I don't think you did anything to Win."

"Then, why are you here?" I asked.

"I'm here because I was asked to find Win," he said, adding, "And you're still the only lead I've got."

"So go to Seattle! Look for him there. . . ."

"Seattle's a big place," he said. "You said so yourself."

"But what if Win can't be found?" I said. "Are you going to keep bugging me until Christmas break, or what?"

He took a deep breath. "I'll find him, Chris. And it's my experience that people like Win generally want to be found—"

"There are no people like Win," I said.

He nodded. "That may be, but I'll find him just the same," he said, adding under his breath, "Coggans will make sure of that."

I remembered his early lie about Win's dad being a friend. Something about him sitting next to me on the bike made him feel less like a scary government investigator and more like just another guy Win's dad was screwing with. A guy like me. "How'd you say you knew him?"

"We were at boarding school together. Years ago. Exeter."

"Goes back that far, huh?" I wondered what indiscretion Mr. Coggans was holding over the FBI agent. Whatever it was, I was certain Ward wasn't making the drive from the federal building downtown just as a favor. "I hope he's slipping you something on the side. What's the going rate for your very own FBI agent, anyway?"

As soon as I said it, I realized I'd crossed a line. His neck flushed red and his eyes narrowed, his whole face sort of clouding up.

"You want to talk about money, Chris? Fine. Let's talk about the money."

I stopped pedaling.

"When I said I didn't think you did anything to Chris, I meant it. But Mr. Coggans isn't so sure."

"That's insane."

"He says you were always jealous of Win's lifestyle. Maybe he's right. I looked into you a bit, Chris. Heavy loans and a dishwashing job in the commons to cover your expenses here at Tech. Wouldn't blame you for being a little envious of Win. I mean, your folks—decent, hardworking. He's a crane operator, right? She still nursing at Saint Mary's? And you. Good athlete, honor society vice president . . ."

Honor society? These guys had way too much time on their hands.

"Eagle Scout, top grades, and only a few small scholarships for your efforts, while Win coasts through high school and gets carte blanche in the Ivy League."

"So what?" I said, trying to hide my alarm that he'd been able to get that much info so easily. "What does that have to do with anything? Half the kids on campus will be paying off loans well into their forties, but you're not accusing them of anything."

He leaned over, looked past me as he whispered, "But you're the only one who just biked cross-country with a guy carrying nineteen thousand dollars in cash when he disappeared."

My foot slipped off the pedal.

"So you want to talk about money, Chris?" he challenged. "Then, talk."

CHAPTER TEN

"I really gotta go, Mom," I said.

"Are you sure you're eating enough?" she asked for the tenth time.

"I'm sure," I repeated.

"Did Gram feed you well?"

"Yeah," I said. If by "well" she meant that everything she served—including the bacon and eggs for breakfast—had been lathered with Miracle Whip.

"I'm just so proud of you, Chris," my mother said. "Riding all that way . . . just so proud. I told everyone at work all about you. Nobody can even believe that my son is riding his bike across America."

"We're only eight days out." Win and I had crossed over this morning into Indiana without even slowing down at the welcome sign. We quickly stopped for lunch and groceries and to call in— something we'd promised to do but hadn't managed to find time for yet.

Win was at the other end of the row of pay phones, leaning against the one he'd just hung up. His conversation had been brief.

"Dad there?" I asked.

"Sure, baby. I'll get him. Postcard, remember?"

"Promise," I said.

Win pushed away from the pay phone and crossed to his bike. He rummaged around for a second before fishing out a giant rubber glove. He'd found it two days ago, and it went all the way up to his bicep when he tugged it on. He turned to face me, affecting his best evil-genius posture.

"What are you doing?" I said to him, covering the mouthpiece with my hand.

"Plotting my strategy for world domination," he said. "First, we need supplies." He strode toward the entrance of the grocery store. "But I can't take over the world without a muscle-bound lackey. Get off the phone and come help me buy cheese, *slave*."

I nodded. "Just a sec."

"The obedient sidekick must not defy his master," Win said.

"I'll keep it in mind."

He gave me a green acidproof thumbs-up and disappeared behind the sliding glass doors of Kroger. There was a muffled sound on the other end of the receiver as my dad picked up the extension.

"Chris?" he said.

"Hey, Dad."

"Okay, Nancy, I've got it, you can hang up now."

Mom air-kissed into the phone before she finally put down the receiver.

"Better make this quick. This phone call's probably costing me a mint," my father said, though I could hear the laughter in his voice.

"I used the calling card, Dad," I said. "So you're in the clear."

"Well, all right. Tell me all about life on the open road, then."

"It's good. And we're eating plenty. I didn't tell Mom, but a couple of days ago we spent two hours in a Shoney's at the salad bar. Then the manager threw us out because we'd bought only one plate and had been sharing it."

He laughed. "What else?"

"Well, we've got this running challenge to jump into any body of water we pass. This morning it was a stinky runoff pond. I still smell, and might sprout a third eye by morning."

He laughed harder. I love hearing my father laugh. "Bike treating you okay?"

"I'm a little sore, but I seem to be breaking into it. A couple more days and I don't think it'll hurt at all."

"Glad to hear it." He paused. "You've got a lot more patience than I have."

"It's all we do every day. Patience is the easy part," I said.

Dad cleared his throat. "Speaking of patience, Chris, I need to ask a favor."

"Anything, Dad."

"I need you to call and check in a little more often."

My dad hated to talk on the phone. "Why?"

"Your mother is making me crazy," he said simply.

"But she sounded fine," I said.

"She talks a good game to everybody else. Brags on you like you'd just won the Nobel Prize or some such, but at home all I get is doom and gloom. Every other minute she's wondering if you're stuck in a ditch or gotten yourself kidnapped."

"Gram said she was going to call for us," I said.

"Oh, she did," Dad countered, "but that made it even worse. Turned into half an hour of worrying about how thin you were and how two boys your age shouldn't be gallivanting all over the country unsupervised."

"Great. Okay, I promise to call in more often. It's just that we're not exactly camping in a lot of places where they have phones."

"Campgrounds don't have phones?" he asked.

"Well, they're not exactly campgrounds. . . . ," I admitted.

"What about the cell phone?"

I hesitated. "Reception's been tricky. And charging it at night has been . . . complicated."

"Say no more. Just find a way."

"Definitely. Twice a week. Would that calm her down?"

"Probably not," he reasoned, "but at least she'll have to give up the kidnapped and dead-in-a-ditch theories."

I laughed. "Thanks for taking the heat, Dad."

"Happy to . . . happy to. Just make sure you write a few of those stories down for your old man," he said.

"Done. Listen, Win's buying the groceries, and if I leave him to it, we'll be eating Doritos and Pixy Stix for the next three days."

He laughed. "Buy something green," he said, "for your mother."

"Thanks, Dad."

"Be safe," he said, and hung up the phone.

I found Win inside with a red plastic basket slung like a fancy handbag over the arm ensconced in the rubber glove.

"This thing's hotter than a mother," he said.

"So take it off," I reasoned.

"No way. It's too funny to be the guy in spandex shorts and the giant glove. This joint will be talking about me for weeks."

I shook my head.

"Check this out," Win said, undaunted, reaching into the basket. He held up two bumper stickers. One said something about not tailgating, the other bore a Mark Twain quote so long that the only way the tiny type could be read was if the car were sitting still.

"What are those for?" I asked.

Win looked at me like I was dense. "The *bikes*?"

"Yeah, because we have bumpers and all," I said.

"We'll figure something out," he said. "Look at these." He handed me a few postcards. "Three for a dollar," he said proudly.

"There's a reason, Win," I said. "These are the dorkiest postcards I've ever seen." I tossed them back into the basket. "And who are you planning to send them to, anyway?"

"I dunno. Be prepared, right, Eagle?" he said, reaching for a small tube. "And I got this, too."

"Krazy Glue? Our patches are self-stick—"

"Not for patching tires, for fixing stuff to the bikes. I'm going to glue my pinkie light and some of my other finds to my top tube . . . or maybe the rack," he said.

Win's Cannondale was not the kind of bike that could be improved upon by gluing junk to it, but I knew better than to argue with him. Besides, the glue might come in handy for other stuff. "Fine," I said, scanning the contents of the basket. Win had managed to pick up bananas, more pasta, a block of cheese, Pop-Tarts, and lunch meat to replace the turkey we'd just finished off.

"Where are the bagels?"

"Bakery's in the back. Haven't gotten there yet. I am, however, a brand-new member of the Kroger savings club," he said, bearing a plastic card meant to be fastened onto a key chain, "and am now entitled to exclusive discounts—we're saving thirty cents on this block of cheddar."

"Well, look who's the Boy Scout now," I said.

"It's the glove. Don't get used to it," he said. "We need anything else?"

"Salsa," I said. "Get in line—I'll go grab a jar and the bagels and meet you up front."

When I rejoined him at the checkout, our items were arranged neatly on the belt, and Win was reading a tabloid. "I'm so relieved to know that the Bat Boy is doing so well," he said, gesturing toward the cover. "They were a little worried about how he'd adjust to junior high, but apparently they made him the mascot and he's a huge hit."

The cashier began pulling our groceries across the scanner, looking bored. I watched the prices pop up on the screen.

"Nineteen dollars and seventy-seven cents," she announced, snapping open a plastic bag.

I reached into the back zippered pocket of my cycling jersey and pulled a ten out of my wallet. I tossed the bill onto the platform next to the credit card scanner and looked at Win. He folded up his magazine. "Yeah . . . I seem to have left my wallet in my other glove." He gestured toward his Dr. No arm. "I'll get the food next time."

"You still owe me for last time too," I said, swapping the bill for a twenty.

"Don't worry, Eagle. I'll take care of it," he said as the clerk handed me my change and Win picked up the bags.

I was annoyed. "You'd better. I'm not spotting you again, loser."

He nodded and carried the bags outside, repeated, "I'll take care of it."

He laid the bags on the pavement. "Gotta pee before we take off. You got this?"

"I'm the muscle-bound lackey who pays all your bills, after all. But I'm giving you the heavy stuff."

"Fair enough," he said, heading back into the store.

I unzipped his rear pannier and shifted a few things around. The bag was full of trash, including a wad of empty grocery sacks. I grabbed the handful and was about to toss them into the garbage when I realized they were heavier than they should be. I untwisted the top of the outermost bag, reached inside, and pulled out a roll of bills as big as a softball, tightly wound with rubber bands. The bill on the outside was a hundred.

"What the . . . ," I started, but didn't finish. My heart thumped. What the heck was all this for?

But instead of waiting to ask him, something made me shove the money back into the bag. I tucked it into his pannier, approximately where he'd had it stashed, and put the jar of salsa and the bagels on top.

I don't know why I put it back. I don't know why I didn't wave it around in his face, or take a couple hundred off in repayment of all the money he'd borrowed, would borrow still. I don't know why I didn't ask him about it when he came back.

"Everything in?" he asked as he came out of the door, pulling off the glove.

I nodded and reached for my helmet.

"I only had to wash one hand," he said proudly, holding up his glove. "Cool, huh?"

I forced a smile. "Hey, when do you think you can pay me back? I'm running a bit low on cash myself," I said.

He unzipped his handlebar bag and fished out his wallet. He snapped it open and withdrew a pair of crumpled one-dollar bills. He held them out to me. "Sorry, man, that's all I've got. We'll find the right ATM tomorrow and I'll give you the rest. My dad's been giving me a hard time about the debit card statements—fees or surcharges or something."

"You can use those cards to actually buy stuff now, you know," I said, unable to look him in the eye as I took the money from his hand.

"Fascinating," he said as he grabbed his helmet. "Don't worry about the money. I'll take care of it. Promise."

I didn't reply as I stepped onto my pedal and pushed away. Win followed, repeating, "Okay?"

I just nodded. I didn't call him on his lie. I didn't flaunt that I knew he had enough cash to keep us living like kings for the rest of the trip. Didn't ask why he had to worry about his dad hassling him all the way out here. And the truth was, I didn't because I was afraid of what I already knew.

CHAPTER ELEVEN

"You never even asked him about the money?" Ward followed me out of the fitness center.

I shook my head.

"Why not?"

"Figured he'd tell me eventually."

Ward sighed. "Chris, he's your best friend. Why didn't he tell you?"

I'd been wondering this myself. "I don't know. Probably the same reason he didn't tell his parents about cleaning out his account. They'd have stopped him. I probably would have tried," I said.

"Why didn't you bring it up with them when you got back?"

"I guess I thought they must have figured it out by then. Or maybe they didn't think it was important."

"That's a pretty major detail to hang on to, Chris," Ward said.

"Then why didn't his parents bring it up?" I asked.

Ward shook his head. "Fair enough," he admitted. We walked several yards before he spoke again. "So, you knew Win better than anyone, even if he didn't tell you. Why would he clean out his savings—nearly twenty grand—in a cash withdrawal the day before your trip?"

I was still stunned by the amount. I'd known holding it in my hand that it had to be somewhere north of ten thousand, but I'd had no idea Win had that much money at his disposal.

"How come the bank even let him take all that money out?" I asked.

"He was eighteen. The account was in his name," Ward said, adding, "But Win's father is asking some questions about that too."

"Asking some questions" probably meant threatening the bank with legal action—or worse, moving his accounts. I doubted his father had any idea how much Win had saved. Though I was surprised, it made sense. When your parents toss guilt money at you, like Win's were prone to, it's probably easy to sock some away.

"But cash?" I said. "Why carry that much around? And with the debit card and all?"

Ward kicked a bottle cap along the sidewalk. "Only a few reasons, really," he said.

"Such as?"

He crossed his arms, looked into the distance. "Well . . . Win was either nuts, engaged in some illegal activity . . ." He paused. "Or he was looking to disappear."

"He isn't crazy, or into drugs," I said.

Ward nodded. "Didn't think so."

"But why does it mean he wanted to disappear?" Though I knew—probably knew the moment I found the money—that Ward was right. "Wouldn't the debit card have left a trail?"

"He quit using it in North Dakota," he said.

Win really had planned ahead.

"You're sure you didn't talk to him about the money, Chris?"

"Not a word."

"Ever collect on a few of those debts without him knowing?" he challenged.

"No way," I said. "He still owes me about seventy-five dollars."

He walked beside me as I headed back to my dorm. Shadows grew longer across the quad in the waning light. Someone was burning leaves somewhere.

"I didn't take his money," I said after a long silence.

He nodded. "I know."

"What else do you know, then?" I asked him.

He scratched his head. "Probably less than you. I have hunches, though. Win had a plan. Wanted to disappear, used the trip as a means to do so. He could have lived on that money for a long while without finding work."

I was struck by how freely he used the past tense. "You mean he could be still," I corrected.

We passed a group of guys kicking a Hacky Sack on the lawn of the student center.

"I don't know, Chris," he said quietly. "Sometimes I get the feeling I'm looking for a ghost. That we're not finding Win because, well, because he's . . ."

"Dead?" I supplied, because he clearly didn't want to say the word. So much for the hard-boiled FBI agent. We walked a dozen yards before he spoke again.

"About ten years back this buddy of mine worked the case on that McCandless kid—the one who took off from his family, cashed out his life savings, quit college, and disappeared. Turned up a couple of years later in Alaska in a school bus he'd been try-ing to use for shelter out in the backcountry. Frozen solid. You hear about that one? Some guy wrote a book about it," Ward said.

Of course. Win had done a book report about it for Kirkland's class a couple years ago. He'd gone on for weeks about that guy, trying to figure out why he did it. "Yeah," I said, "Win tried all tenth grade to get me to read that stupid book."

"I wish I was more surprised," Ward said.

I nodded, unsure whether he meant he already knew—like he'd known about honor society.

"Then, I have a really hard time believing it's all coincidental. Here's Win—from a wealthy family, with a load of cash, a good education waiting for him—probably engineering this little escape from the start. The stories are awfully similar."

"But that doesn't mean they necessarily end the same way," I said, my voice cracking, surprising even me with the emotion. Ward pretended not to notice.

We reached the parking lot of my dorm, where Ward had a parking ticket slapped on the windshield of his black sedan. "Maybe you're right, Chris."

"But you don't think so?"

"I think he escaped—one way or the other," he said, pulling

the ticket from the windshield and unlocking the car. "I'll be in touch."

I watched him drive away, trying to make real in my mind that Win was more than just gone.

Could Win really be dead? It had of course been among the possibilities, but I hadn't paid much attention to it before. It was sort of the option on a multiple-choice question that you dismiss first because it can't possibly be the right answer. But then when you go through all the other choices, they don't fit either.

But dead? No way. Not Win.

I was still wondering this as I jammed my room key into the mailbox slot and opened the door to reveal a large manila envelope from my mom. I broke the seal with my key on the way to my room. Inside the package I found a note from Mom, my mail from home, and the packet of photos she'd picked up from the developers.

I hadn't seen pictures of the trip yet. When Win disappeared, he took the record of our trip with him. But I'd taken photos here and there along our route with those disposable cameras I'd packed. I'd always meant to mail them home when they got full, but they didn't really fill up as fast as I'd figured, since we mainly used Win's camera. And only one of mine had survived the trip.

The pictures were a random highlight reel of stuff I hadn't really thought much about. There was one of Win riding past the Iowa state line sign I'd shot as I rode behind him, a detour we'd decided to take just so we could add another state to the list of ones we'd ridden in. We camped at this state park called Effigy

Mounds, where apparently a bunch of Native Americans had buried themselves and their stuff. I remember being pretty impressed, but in the few photos it just looked like a random field covered in grassy little hills.

Then there was the giant Paul Bunyan statue in Minnesota, complete with his blue ox sidekick. The photo showed them both from a wide angle, Win beneath the ox to see if Babe was male or female. We'd debated on this point.

A shot of a collection of old rusted cars randomly placed by the roadside. I'd taken a picture because it was the first thing of interest we'd seen in two days of riding through the mind-numbing landscape of North Dakota. Plus, old beat-up cars in somebody's field made me a little nostalgic for West Virginia.

The pictures were nothing like the trip. Nothing like what we'd done or felt or seen out there. I wondered if Win's were any more real.

I tucked them back into the envelope and reached for the stack of postcards. The sight of them made me temporarily forget that my oldest friend might be dead and that I was under investigation. Four postcards, all from girls we'd met on the road.

At home neither of us had ever had a girlfriend. But on the road it actually seemed possible. "Women love us," Win had remarked one day as we left a Dairy Queen where a cute girl named Shayna had been sneaking us refills on soft-serve ice cream for the last several hours because we made her laugh.

It was true that biking cross-country was a good conversation starter. True that we seemed instantly cool, since we were doing something that everybody wished they could. I saw myself not as all the girls I'd gone to high school with saw me—that is, one of the two skinny dorks who were always laughing at something stupid. For the first time we were cool, and we knew it.

Four girls across the country, spread out like a bread-crumb trail. Annie in Indiana—funny redhead we'd spent most of an evening with when we crashed her family reunion in a city park. Sarah from Minnesota, who'd been forced to listen to our stories while confined to her lifeguard stand at a city pool. Lifeguards were always Win's favorites. Jessica in North Dakota. Jessica. The girl we met in a 7-Eleven parking lot who sang us the song she'd performed at the Miss Eastern North Dakota pageant (second runner-up) and pretty much made me fall in love with her in a few short hours. Hers was postmarked from the state university where she was a freshman, like me. All three postcards had *x*'s and *o*'s beneath curvy signatures—the closest I'd ever get to making out with any of them.

The fourth was different.

The handwriting was loopy and wildly uneven. Then I noticed the signature. It wasn't a signature at all, but a set of letters—all cut from the same source, by the look of them—glued to the card. A corner of the last letter peeled away. I tugged nervously at the loose edge as I read the message.

chris,
Hope you're enjoying school and
that you made it back okay.
Budweiser remains the number
one choice of litterbugs.
Thought you'd like to know.

Your friend,

tricksey

PS: I really thought our time
together this summer was pretty
special.

Who the hell was Tricksey? I checked the postmark. She was somewhere in Montana. The Budweiser reference didn't help. Win and I had shared that bit of insight with probably a hundred people, most of them girls our age we were trying to impress with our road knowledge.

But Tricksey? And if our time had been so special, why hadn't she bothered to give me a return address on the card?

I thought about going for my journal but knew it wouldn't be much help. I'd written maybe half a dozen pages the entire trip, in spite of my promise to my dad.

Tricksey.

Girls tend to travel in packs, and Win and I often ran into them in large groups. I'd sucked with the names, usually only remembering the cutest one or the one who seemed most willing to carry the conversation. Tricksey may have been one of those background girls. They were pretty easy to forget.

I flipped the card over and stared at the front. WISH YOU WERE HERE! it declared, the message hovering above a collection of random items, including a cardinal and a fat red flower that looked like a rose on steroids. In smaller letters below, it invited me to visit the Hoosier State.

I wished I'd thought to take pictures of all the people we'd met. I chucked the postcards and photos onto my desk and started to walk away, but something made me reach out and grab the mysterious one from Tricksey. I studied it again, trying to divine meaning from the random doodles of flowers and stars framing the words. Who was she?

Somehow I convinced myself that if I stared at it long enough, I'd remember. But it was just like those pathetic photos. No matter how long I looked at them, they weren't going to match up to what it was like out there. I was probably better off imagining this girl. Reality had a disappointing habit of not measuring up to my memories.

CHAPTER TWELVE

"Isn't Illinois supposed to be flatter than this?" Win complained as I followed him up another hill.

"I don't know," I said, standing on my pedals for extra leverage, rocking the bike side to side, panniers drifting just a few inches from the pavement. "Do you think we made a wrong turn? Ended up in Arkansas or something?"

I felt strong. We'd made good time through Indiana, and each day I ached a little less when we started our morning ride. We were moving so fast we decided to veer toward Iowa to follow the Mississippi up a ways before heading due west again.

And last night we'd gotten an unexpectedly good night's sleep after scamping just outside Freeport—self-proclaimed pretzel capital of the world and home to about nine thousand Abraham Lincoln statues.

My quads now strained slightly at the elastic of my bike shorts—the beginnings of the first real muscle I'd ever had on my legs. Two weeks and a thousand miles on a Trek will do that. Sadly, the arms were not keeping up. To compensate, we had nightly push-up contests, or pull-up challenges if we scamped close enough to a playground with monkey bars.

Win ranted on. "Land of Ten Thousand Lakes, right? Well, how'd all the lakes get here if these hills are in the way?

"Ow!" he shouted, slapping his calf as his tirade continued. "And nobody ever mentions the mosquitoes. If they were really going to be honest, they'd have to say Land of Ten Thousand Lakes and Ten Billion Mosquitoes. And where are all the cows? Shouldn't we be seeing, like, acres of cheese out there or something?" he said, gesturing toward a cornfield.

"Wisconsin has cheese. Minnesota has lakes. This is Illinois, idiot," I said.

"What do they have?" he asked.

"Lincoln," I said, adding, "and the Blues Brothers."

I laughed, but then I heard a sudden hiss of air as my back wheel wobbled. "Flat," I called out automatically.

"Front or back?"

I dismounted and stood next to my bike. "Back. Ready?" I asked him.

He pushed a button on his Timex, looked at me. "Are *you* ready?"

I nodded.

My relationship with Win walks a fine line between friendship and rivalry. When two guys have been friends as long as we have, almost everything becomes an opportunity for competition. Out on the road those contests took on new forms. The push-ups. The cheddar challenge—in which we dared each other to eat whole blocks of off-brand processed cheese without throwing up. Hell, we'd been arguing a couple of days ago about whose bike-glove tan was worse.

But despite the fact that we spent the bulk of our days on the bikes, we never raced. It seemed understood that this crossing was something bigger than even our friendship or our rivalry. It was a *partnership*. Still, I had noticed that over the last two weeks we'd been stretching the imaginary line that connected our two bikes as we rode. Seemed through Ohio we stayed within a dozen feet of each other. Now we were slowly spreading out, sometimes riding for an hour or more maybe ten or fifteen yards apart, without talking. But we always finished our days side by side somehow.

That didn't mean that other aspects of cycling were immune from competition.

Win hit the timer. "Go."

I sprang to action, took off my right rear pannier, and laid my bike on its side. The air wasn't escaping anymore now that there was no weight on the tire. I undid the quick release, extracted the wheel from the chain and then reached into my pannier pocket for the plastic tire irons. I unsnapped them from each other and laid them aside. Carefully I rotated the tire, poring over its surface.

"Got it," I said, using my thumb and forefinger to pinch out a sliver of amber-colored glass.

"Nothing beats a cold Budweiser," Win intoned, "unless it's the poetry of throwing the empty bottle from the window of a jacked-up pickup with a gun rack."

I grabbed my irons, inserted the narrow ends a few inches on either side of the puncture, and slid them sideways to lever the rubber tire off the rim. With practiced precision I pulled out the section of the tube and dropped a mouthful of spit onto the area where I'd recovered the glass. I didn't even slow down to wipe the stringer off my chin.

"So gross, dude," Win said.

"But it works," I crowed as I pressed the tube slightly and watched the bubbles form around the puncture. I dried it quickly with an orphaned sock that had spilled from my bag, and snatched the sandpaper from my repair kit. I roughed the tube carefully in two directions, grabbed one of the precut patches, peeled off the adhesive backing, and pressed it in place, holding for a ten count.

"Too long," Win said, glancing at his watch. "You'll never make it!"

I ignored him, slipped the tube inside the tire, fed the edge back into the rim, and grabbed my pump from where it was strapped beneath the length of my crossbar. I uncapped the valve on the tire, fitted the nozzle, and began sliding the shaft back and forth to fill the tire with air.

"Remind you of anything?" Win asked.

"Pervert," I said, paying close attention to the growing tension in the tire. When I was satisfied with the pressure, I recapped the tube, stowed my gear, and grabbed the wheel, threading it carefully back into the rear fork and the chain. Then I tightened the quick release, righted my bike, repositioned my panniers, and shouted, "Time!"

Win hit the button on his watch. "Impressive. Two minutes and sixteen seconds. I think that's a new record for rear-tire flat replacement," he said.

"You know it is," I said, fixing my left foot into my pedal.

"At least I'm still safe with the front record," he said, following suit.

"For now." I took the lead. The hill leveled out just beyond the spot where I'd blown the flat, cresting with a covered wooden bridge spanning a bright, still river.

"I think my shrink has that painting," Win said.

"Looks like somebody's going to come out and offer us a lemonade or something," I said.

We hadn't seen a car in half an hour. Our wheels switched from pavement to the worn timbers of the bridge floor, and the bikes bounced along between the ruts. The sides of the bridge were partially open to the air, with a low wall rising about two feet off the floor. Support posts stood sentry every ten feet or so down the length.

We stopped in the middle of the bridge and looked down.

"That the Mississippi?" Win asked me.

"No. Not until we get to the state line. This is just a creek. Probably flows in, though," I said.

"Didn't think so. It doesn't look mighty enough," he said quietly.

I nodded. "But it looks pretty deep."

"And we do have that thing about jumping into water," he said back.

I judged the distance. "What is that? Maybe thirty feet down?"

Win nodded. We both watched the current flow silently beneath us for a full minute.

"We really should, shouldn't we?" I said.

Win reached for his helmet, unclipped it, and hooked it on his handlebars. "It'd be a crime not to."

Within seconds we had removed T-shirts, shoes, and socks and were standing on the opposite side of the low wall, staring down at the water.

"It seems higher now," Win said.

"You want to go first?"

"No, you."

"On three, then?"

Win nodded.

"One," he said.

We edged closer to the drop, loosened our grip on the beams beside us.

"Two," I said, but before I could think, Win was already halfway to the water.

"Chicken!" he yelled a split second before disappearing in a splash of muddy green.

"Bastard," I muttered as I stepped out into nothing and let the creek rush up to meet me.

CHAPTER THIRTEEN

I'd been carrying that postcard around with me since yesterday, but I hadn't had much time to devote to who Tricksey might be. Classes were already piling on work, and washing dishes twelve hours a week was proving soggy and exhausting. And now my adviser had requested a meeting with me. Yesterday I'd received an e-mail asking me to meet him in his office. Since I hadn't even taken a quiz yet, I couldn't imagine what he wanted.

I reached the College of Engineering building at the heart of the old campus and descended the stairs to his basement office. I knew the place—I'd spent time here when my parents brought me for a campus visit last spring, and again during orientation, making sure my classes were in order. Both times I'd found it a little stifling, sitting as Halverson laid out what my future at Tech would look like—exactly how many nonscience classes I'd have room for in my schedule after I got my general ed requirements out of the way. The prospect of more of that, or him trying to make me feel bad for already falling behind, was adding a new ingredient to the anger-worry-panic cocktail I'd been stewing in: envy.

But I arrived on time and stepped toward the open door, slowing as I heard two voices coming from inside. I recognized Halverson's gravelly drawl, but another accent cut through, even more familiar. It couldn't be. . . .

But it was. There in Dr. Halverson's office sat Winston Coggans II, sipping at a paper coffee cup and laughing at something Halverson had said.

"Mr. Collins," Dr. Halverson said as I stood gaping in the doorway.

"I . . ."

"Hello, Chris," Mr. Coggans said, eyeing me from his seat.

"Hi," I managed.

Dr. Halverson looked nervous, despite the fact that I'd heard them laughing moments before. "I had no idea you and Winston's son were such good friends," he said, looking from my face to Mr. Coggans's.

"Um, yeah," I said, wondering if this was Coggans's way of nailing me for ignoring his e-mail.

"Titan Chemical has been a major supporter of the engineering college. They host a great many of our co-op students every year. They even offer a competitive scholarship for chemical engineering majors," he said.

"Really?" I said, easing into a chair on the opposite side of the small office. I hugged my backpack to my chest.

"You mean you didn't know of the connection when you applied?" he asked, looking at me in a way that made me know he was worried he'd underestimated my importance. "Mr. Coggans tells me you and his boy have been the best of friends for years." Then he turned to Win's father.

"You still should have sent him here, I say. Where did he end up, anyway?"

Win's father hesitated a moment, shot me a quick glance. "Dartmouth."

"Well, I suppose that's all right," Halverson said, smiling. Win's father hadn't told him. Of course he hadn't told him. When no one spoke again for what seemed an inappropriate length of time, Halverson stood abruptly.

"Well, I've got another meeting," he said.

"What about our appointment?" I asked.

He looked at me blankly. "I don't need to speak with you. Mr. Coggans asked me to summon you here. He thought it might be a nice surprise to see a familiar face during this transition period. I agreed," he said, though his tone sounded more like he wondered what the hell was going on.

"Yeah," I said quietly. "Nice."

Halverson looked almost apologetic. "Well, I'll leave you the room. Winston," he said, extending his hand, "always a pleasure."

"Likewise," said Win's father, shaking his hand.

"And stop by if you need anything, Chris. Anything at all. My door is always open."

He hadn't been that friendly when I was here before with my parents or on my own during orientation. Win's dad had him spooked.

He hurried from the office and left the two of us sitting in silence. A Frisbee sailed into the glass of the closed window, making me jump. A muffled "Sorry, dude" followed. And then Mr. Coggans spoke.

"I paid for the restorations to this building, you know," he said, looking around at the books and diplomas on the wall of Halverson's office.

"It's nice," I said. What was I supposed to say to a man who was clearly trying to show me how much he owned? Including my school and professors?

"Are you finding your classes challenging?"

"Um, yeah," I said, adding, "Among other things."

He hesitated again before standing to deposit his coffee cup in the garbage. Then he leaned against the desk. "Hope you don't mind me stopping by. I had business here in Atlanta. The company pilot was kind enough to hold the return flight at my request."

He paused. He still hadn't told me why he was here, but of course I knew.

He continued. "Thank you for your discretion about Win," he said.

I nodded before he went on. "We're intent on keeping the circle of people as small as possible for as long as we can."

"That makes sense, I guess." I'd never even been around Mr. Coggans when Win wasn't present, much less tried to have a conversation with him.

"And Abe Ward tells me you've been very cooperative so far," he said, pausing again and waiting for a challenge.

"He seems to trust you," he added, watching me for some reaction. I wondered again what it might have been like to grow up with him for a father. What it must have been like for Win. What it might feel like to always worry about saying the wrong thing at the wrong moment.

"He said you think I did something to Win," I said, adding, "For his money."

He sighed and shook his head. "I'm sure you appreciate how concerned Win's mother and I are. It may be hard to understand if you're not a parent, but imagine how many questions you'd have, how many theories you'd test out if any of them might lead you to find your son. We're very worried."

"Me too," I said.

He weighed that for a moment. "And your parents have been very supportive as well."

"They like Win a lot," I said.

"So I'm sure you'll understand why I've taken certain measures of late to . . . to try and speed the process along."

I nodded. "I guess I'd do whatever I could to find Win if I were you," I said. This was a side of Coggans I'd never really seen before. I'd only seen the one that yelled at Win or acted annoyed with him. Even at the meeting between our parents after I got back alone, he'd been sort of businesslike and official, trying to establish timelines and exactly what had happened, more like the guy who'd written me that e-mail.

"I apologize if you've felt put on the spot, but . . . Win's mother and I are getting desperate. She's having a very difficult time," he said. Allowing me space to imagine what that might mean for her. "We're told that there's a limited window of sorts in situations like these. The further you get from the last sighting, the more the chance of a successful recovery diminishes."

Despite his careful, professional choice of words, his voice seemed to falter a little. I sneaked a glance at his face. The folds of skin beneath his eyes were shadowy, and his hair had grown a little longer than I'd ever seen it. I was beginning to feel sorry for him.

"Win's not as mature as you are, Chris. He wouldn't do well out there on his own. The only reason I let him go was because he was with you."

I didn't know whether to be flattered or indignant on Win's behalf.

"Oh, he's a bright boy, but he never applied himself. He'll allow himself to be taken advantage of. Or anger the wrong people. He enjoys his own antics, but other people tend to tire pretty quickly of his little tricks," he said.

"Yeah, but on the trip . . . ," I began, before a thought came screaming at me sideways, derailing my reply.

Tricks.

Tricksey. The Hobbit reference from the first day of our trip.

Win was alive.

Win had sent that postcard. Even the handwriting was familiar now. I'd seen Win write left-handed cursive all through school, imitating his mother's signature for report cards and disciplinary notices. I was sure that's what he'd done on that card. I must have jumped or nodded or something, because Mr. Coggans's voice brought me back to myself.

"Chris?" he said.

"Sorry," I said, my cheeks burning. "I was just trying to think if I've forgotten anything."

He eyed me carefully. "As I was saying, I only tell you this so you understand that Win's safe return is the sole objective here," he said.

Win was alive. Or had been when he sent me that card. I tried to remember the date on the postmark. It couldn't have been more than a week or so ago. Unless it had been at Mom and Dad's for a while, waiting for me. He probably hadn't bothered to find my address here before sending it. Or maybe he thought it was somehow safer to send it to my house.

I tried to pay attention to Mr. Coggans, but the postcard in the pocket of my pack seemed to be calling out to me. I could hand it over to him now. He'd give it to the FBI, and they would use it to find Win somehow. Everybody could stop freaking out. I could get on with my life. I could stop worrying about Win and let someone else take care of him for a change.

"We only want him home safe," his father repeated.

"What about getting him back for school?" I asked.

"That's secondary at this point. And in light of recent events, I'm not sure he's ready to be away at college. He might need to spend some more time at home, or in a place where he can learn some discipline, before he's allowed to make these kinds of choices again."

"Discipline?" I asked.

He ignored me. "So you'll understand that I'm prepared to take this to the next level."

"The next level?" Why was I only able to repeat what he was saying?

He leaned over me. "I don't believe you killed my son. But you can't expect me to believe that Win hasn't contacted you."

The postcard wasn't begging to be handed over anymore. If anything, I could picture it slipping deeper into the tangle of junk in the pocket of my pack. "Contacted how? You can check my e-mail or phone records if you want. He hasn't tried to reach me." I paused, then added, "Mr. Coggans," while studying a chipped corner of the tile beneath my feet.

After a beat he spoke again. "Be careful, Chris. I think you've seen enough to know what I can do here."

I had. I'd seen him yell at a senator. I'd seen how nervous he made my adviser. I'd seen him chip away at Win for the last ten years. I knew exactly what he could do.

"Where is he?" he demanded.

I shook my head. "I don't know. All I know is what I told you. We've been over what happened that last day a hundred times. . . ."

More details about the postcard began to knit themselves together. Those letters must have been cut from those stupid bumper stickers he'd bought that day in the grocery store. He never did figure out how to attach them to his bike. And the card was probably one of the ones he'd bought that day. And the "special time" reference was classic Win.

"I'm going to ask that question once more. Before you answer, I want you to consider what you've seen so far. The FBI, your professor, my access to you here at your school . . . those are just the tip of what I can do, Chris. You've no idea the resources at my disposal. So before you answer, weigh carefully what you're prepared to sacrifice for my son."

I couldn't breathe. Couldn't think. Couldn't speak. The bell tower in the quad pealed. I popped up.

"Where is my son?" he asked, his voice sounding desperate now instead of threatening.

"I have to go," I said, bolting for the door.

Coggans's voice followed me out. "I'll expect to hear from you soon, Chris," he said. "There's only so long I'll wait, you understand."

I did. Perfectly. I understood I couldn't let him know about the postcard. Not yet. As angry as I was at Win, as afraid of his father as I was now, there were answers I needed. Something told me that if I shared that postcard with anybody else, I wasn't likely to get them.

CHAPTER FOURTEEN

"You know, they'd get a lot more visitors back in Pepin if they had more interesting crap in the gift shop," Win said as he rode beside me in the gathering dark.

"Stop talking about it," I muttered, tugging down on the zipper of my rain jacket. "It's bad enough you conned me into it. Now have the decency to at least let me block the memory."

It was nearly nine o'clock and I was starving. I was still wearing my rain jacket from this morning, the first time I'd tugged it out of my pannier since we left. Clouds swelled above us. We'd seen very little rain throughout the trip, and even that was usually so brief and violent we could wait it out for a few minutes before hopping back on our bikes. But this morning, after riding only eight miles or so after breakfast, the rain opened up and left us stranded in Pepin, Wisconsin, birthplace of that lady who wrote *Little House on the Prairie*. Apparently Win had been a closet fan of the TV show based on the book.

"I still can't believe you watched that crap," I said to Win as I swerved left around a puddle that had gathered in the gravel shoulder of Highway 35.

"Only reruns when I was sick," he said. "That girl that played Laura had these crazy teeth when she was a kid, but she was hot when she got older."

"The museum would probably be a lot more popular if they had her around, then," I said.

"And pig-bladder beach balls in the gift shop," he added quickly.

I'd let Win talk me into paying two bucks for the only qualifying tourist attraction in Pepin—a reproduction of a log-cabin pioneer homestead. The only interesting trivia that Win picked up was that when Pa Ingalls used to slaughter a hog, he'd make a balloon out of the bladder. He was so impressed by this fact that he asked the nervous little old man volunteering in the small gift shop if they kept pig bladders in stock.

We ate lunch at ten thirty in the morning as the rain ran in sheets off the edge of the cabin roof. As soon as the torrent eased, we hopped back onto our bikes and began riding, intent on making up the miles we'd sort of wasted the past few days. We'd been moving kind of slowly, leapfrogging back and forth over the Mississippi as we made our way north from Iowa into Wisconsin, angling north toward Route 2, the road we planned to follow for our big westward push. We went swimming a lot. Stayed a night with this really nice family we met outside the library, and generally cut back on our mileage as we goofed off. We'd vowed today would be different, but the weather hadn't been part of our agreement.

Riding in the rain was vastly more appealing than covered wagons and calico, but it had been a long day. Now the oily pavement still glistened beneath the streetlights. My jacket stuck to my arms beneath, wet on the outside by rain, and inside by sweat from cycling hard with an extra layer on. The temperature had been dropping, and steam rose off my legs as I stroked down on my pedals. If I stopped riding, I might actually be cold for the first time on the trip.

Sixty miles now lay between us and Pepin, but it was getting dark and we needed a place to sleep. More importantly, we needed a place to let the bikes dry out a bit so we could reoil the chains and gears in the morning. That meant we'd need to find a city park or a picnic shelter we could crash in.

"So, you think Hudson's going to have anything half as cool as Pepin?" Win asked.

I shrugged. "Doesn't matter. We can't go any farther in the dark. And we need food."

He nodded. A few miles back, we passed under the interstate that led to Minneapolis. The presence of a bigger city meant that even on back roads, night traffic couldn't be counted on to dry up like it did when we were in more rural areas.

"Sleep here in Hudson, right?" Win said, pointing at the green-and-white road sign announcing the city limit.

"Have to," I said. "Even though I don't see anything on the

map for a campground in town. There's a state park and a lake about five miles farther out, but we don't have enough light to make it. We'll have to figure something out."

"Scamping?"

I nodded. "Yeah. But it might be tricky," I said, surveying the quiet streets. "Town looks pretty packed in. They'd notice a tent just about anywhere."

"No real chance of meeting anybody this late who'll take us in," he pointed out.

Most of the storefronts were closed, and only a few windows of houses flickered from television light inside. "Wait here," I told Win as I turned into the city park, scanning for a dark corner where we could hide, or a building where we might be able to set up the tent and maybe even keep the bikes from getting any wetter. Nothing. Even the playground was in full view of the main street.

I circled back to find Win where I'd left him. But he wasn't alone.

A St. Croix County sheriff's car was idling beside him, Win leaning over his handlebars, talking to the cop seated inside.

I shook my head. Great. On top of everything else Win had gotten himself pulled over. On a *bike*. I rode over, hoping I wasn't too late to keep Win from pissing off the law.

"Hey," I said nervously as I braked next to him.

"Chris!" said Win. "I was just explaining to Deputy Lindt the day we've had and how we're looking for a place to sleep."

The deputy stepped out of the car. He couldn't have been more than four or five years older than we were. Skinny as me too.

"State park's sort of full," he said. "Bass Fishing Derby this week."

I nodded. "Too far for us to make tonight anyway," I said, relieved that Win wasn't working on getting himself thrown in jail.

"So he called in on the radio, and they said they have a spot for us down in front of the station," Win said.

"That way we can keep an eye on you . . . look out for you . . . that sort of thing," Lindt said.

"Great," I said.

Win smiled.

The deputy climbed back into his car. "Follow me," he said. He drove slowly through the town center, giving Win and me plenty of time to keep up.

"Nicely done," I said to Win.

"Yeah. I figured instead of trying to dodge the cops, maybe asking for a change might work. Protect and serve, right?"

"I just never figured you for the law-abiding type," I said as we rolled through a four-way and followed the cruiser two more blocks away from the river to a small brick building.

"It is Eagle territory, I admit," he said, "but I can fake it."

We pulled up behind the cruiser as Lindt emerged, a wry smile on his face. "I just got off the line with the sheriff," he said.

"Are we in trouble now?" I asked.

The deputy laughed. "No. He said it was fine if you guys camped on the lawn here. But he also said you can have the empty holding cell if you want."

I didn't process what he was saying at first. "Excuse me?"

He smiled. "This place is like Mayberry, you know?" he said, his accent growing more pronounced as he relaxed. "My uncle's the sheriff. He said if you wanted, I could put you in the empty cell, and you could have the bunks and even take your bikes inside the garage. Your gear's probably soaked."

"Um, yeah," I said, still trying to get my head around staying a night in a jail cell.

"Sounds perfect," Win said as he stepped off his bike and unclasped his helmet.

Lindt nodded and said something about heading in to open it up. He pointed us toward an open garage door and instructed us to stow our bikes inside.

"Are you sure this is such a good idea?" I asked Win when we were out of earshot.

He stopped and turned to me, his face only half illuminated by the light spilling from the garage into the small parking lot. "It's more than a good idea," he began, "it's necessary. As your best friend, it's my job to make sure you take advantage of an opportunity like this. You will never again see the inside of a jail cell, Eagle," he said solemnly. "We both know that it's likely I may once again spend a night in the slammer—rich men's sons are obligated to get at least a DUI or something. My dad would probably be disappointed if I didn't. But I won't allow you to let *your* moment pass you by."

"Yeah, but he said the *empty* cell," I pointed out. "That means that the others are, you know, *not empty*."

Win considered this for a moment. "Well, I doubt they'd let us sleep next to a murderer or anything. The guy probably just has a bunch of unpaid parking tickets," he said. "I mean, look at this place. Do you really think they're going to keep hardened criminals in there?"

He was right. The outside of the little brick building did look pretty much like a regular house, except for the size and infrequency of the windows, crisscrossed with reinforcing wire. And the garage was occupied by only one police car and a bunch of normal garage stuff: a few basketballs, a lawn mower, and some random tools.

"Plus, it's too dark to ride on any farther," he said, pushing his bike the rest of the way in. "And this way we can save time and make up the difference tomorrow when we don't have to pack up the tent."

"Yeah, but—"

Just then a door at the top of a pair of concrete steps squeaked open and Lindt appeared. "C'mon in, fellas," he said to us, before shouting over his shoulder, "Cedric! Toto! Clean this place up! You've got company!"

Win turned to me. "*Cedric* and *Toto*. Don't they sound like fun? Maybe you'll even get a prison nickname," he whispered as he sprang up the steps and into the hallway.

I wondered how long I'd wait before I told my mother about this night—if I ever had a chance—but I followed Win up the steps anyway. Inside a small kitchen area were two guys wearing orange coveralls. The first guy was a head shorter than me, but thick and square. His hair stuck out at funky angles, and he blinked his eyes repeatedly in the fluorescent light. "I'm Cedric," he said, extending a hand covered in small, fuzzy tattoos. One outline was of a dagger. "He's Toto," he said, gesturing toward the bigger guy, who merely nodded and sat back down in a folding chair before turning up the volume on the action movie he was watching.

"No manners, that one," the deputy said. "Cedric, show these guys where the shower is. Toto, wash those dishes. You guys gotta clean up after yourselves. We have to have some kind of order around here." Lindt sounded a little embarrassed at the condition, and maybe the comfort, of his prisoners. I was still trying to figure out what the hell these guys could have done to deserve a prison term where they apparently cooked their own meals and watched cable all night.

Cedric led us to a small closet at the end of the hall. "Shower," he announced, pulling open the heavy metal door. The inside was like a large phone booth, a nozzle poking out of one wall above a single metal button. "Gotta push this to make the water come out. No hot or cold. Just warm. Wear shoes," he said pointing at the floor. "Toto's got wicked fungus on his foot. Guy's nasty," he said, reaching for a pair of white towels on a rack outside the door.

"Thanks," I said.

"You guys eat?" he asked me.

I shook my head.

"Burger drive-in around the corner's open till midnight. They deliver, but we walk up there sometimes too. It's like a knockoff White Castle, but better. Get a whole bag of little cheeseburgers for, like, four bucks," he said.

"Okay," I said, wondering again what kind of place this was.

"Listen, my wife's waiting on me to call her, and then I'm

going to turn in early," he announced. "Toto and me gotta take the cruisers to the car wash tomorrow, and then we mow down by the city building."

"Thanks for your help," Win said.

"Turn down the damn TV, Toto!" Cedric yelled as he passed by the open lounge area. He disappeared at the other end of the hall behind a door with a huge bolt on the outside and what looked like a big mail slot about chest high.

Deputy Lindt poked his head out of the room next door. "In here, guys," he said. Win and I entered the cell. It was about the size of my bedroom at home. A pair of small sealed windows hovered a few inches from the ceiling. One wall held two bunks, braced against cinder blocks painted a sickly shade of greenish gray. The opposite wall had a small, low toilet without a real seat to speak of. The white porcelain was chipped, and rust marked the areas near the bolts that secured it to the floor. Where the tank might have been on a normal toilet there was a grimy little sink with a single knob and faucet.

"I keep telling Chris we ought to figure out some way to pull something like this along behind us on our bikes," Win said, surveying the toilet-sink combo like a museum piece.

Lindt smiled. "I know it looks gross, but it's clean. We make the guys disinfect and everything," he said. "Mattresses, too." He gestured toward the green vinyl rectangles on the flat metal shelves that would serve as our beds. "You guys got sleeping bags, right?"

"Yeah. This will be great," Win said.

With little else to say, he nodded his acknowledgment. "Feel free to spread your gear out in the garage if you need to dry stuff out," he said. "I've got to head back out on patrol. Not that anything's going to happen in Hudson. Nothing ever really does."

"We were thinking of going to get some of those cheap burgers," I said.

Lindt nodded. "Tell 'em I sent you. He'll toss in the fries for free."

"You are well connected," Win joked.

Lindt smiled again and stepped outside the cell. He pointed to the bolt. "Locks on the outside. Oscar—the guy on the desk tonight—will lock up Cedric and Toto when the movie's over. I'll tell him to leave your door open."

"That'd be great," Win said.

Lindt nodded and started to walk away, one hand trailing on the doorframe. "All the way from West Virginia, huh?" he asked.

Win nodded. Lindt shook his head. "Wish I had time to hear about it," he said, tapping the door frame with his fist and then disappearing.

An hour later Win and I had eaten our way through a paper sack full of greasy hamburgers and both taken our turn in the shower stall. We'd hung up our wet clothes in the garage and set a few things out to dry before returning to our cell. Win sat on the lower bunk, holding a pen and one of the postcards he'd bought back in Indiana. "Who should I write to?"

"I don't care, Win," I said. All I wanted was to go to sleep.

"Seriously. Don't all those great people write letters from jail and stuff? You know . . . Emerson, Martin Luther King . . . the ones we read in American Lit."

"They were in jail because they were wrongly imprisoned. We're in jail because you thought it would be fun," I pointed out. "You're not likely to end up on anyone's reading list anytime soon."

"Just tell me who to write to," he said.

"Your parents."

"No, really," he said, poking my mattress from beneath with his pen.

"*Really*, I don't care," I said, trying to adjust my sleeping bag beneath me so my skin wasn't in contact with the mattress. I stuck to the plastic, but my bag kept sliding all over the place. Between that, the volume of Toto's current movie choice, and the smell of disinfectant, I was starting to think that this wasn't going to work.

"Fine. I'll write to your mom and tell her about life in the joint," he said.

"Leave my mom alone. Torment your own," I said, turning toward the wall.

Suddenly the lights snapped off and the TV went quiet. "Curfew," called Oscar, the night deputy we'd met on our way in from dinner. Toto's metal chair scraped along the floor, then I heard him stand and shuffle back to his cell. A moment later keys jingled on a belt as Oscar came behind and locked it up. Then he stopped at our door. "You guys okay?"

"Great," Win said.

"Let me know if you need anything," Oscar replied.

"You bet," Win said in the darkness.

The footsteps died away.

I was almost asleep. One of the guys next door farted. "Did you ever dream when we were back in the physics closet at school that we'd someday be sleeping in a jail cell in Hudson, Wisconsin?" Win asked.

I ignored him.

"I mean, it's kind of epic, you know? Bike trip magic."

"Go to sleep, Win," I said.

"Yeah . . . okay," he said.

I didn't sleep well. I had to readjust the sleeping bag beneath me, and halfway through the night one of the guys next door must have lit a cigarette, because smoke poured through a hidden vent and into our cell. When I heard a different deputy shout back at Cedric and Toto to get up, I was relieved that day had arrived and I had fulfilled my obligation to take advantage of this life experience.

"That was the crappiest I've slept the whole trip," I said, sitting up and rubbing my eyes.

Win didn't reply. I hopped down, my bag slipping to the floor behind me. I turned to Win's bunk.

It was empty.

I looked around the tiny cell. Empty.

I couldn't put words to what I was worried about. What I thought might have happened. It was a little bit like finding all that money. I stepped quickly into my shoes and tossed my sleeping bag over my shoulder. "Win?" I called out as I pulled open the door.

The lounge and hallway were empty. I could hear Cedric and Toto stirring in their room.

I bolted through the hall and into the garage. Something in me expected to find his bike missing. But it was there, and so was he.

Win was spread out on the floor, his ground pad unrolled, asleep next to the bikes.

My heart slowed.

I walked over and toed him in the elbow with my shoe. "What the hell are you doing out here?" I asked, stuffing my sleeping bag back into its sack.

Win threw his forearm across his eyes. "Sleeping. I couldn't in there. The smell or the air was getting to me."

"You should have told me," I said.

"You were asleep," he pointed out.

"But you could have left a note."

"Chris, I went, like, thirty feet," he said.

I shook my head. "Scared straight, then?" I said, switching my Tevas for my biking shoes.

"Something like that," he said. "Early start? Pop-Tarts on the road?"

"Breakfast of champions," I said, shoving the stuff we'd laid out last night back into panniers. Win sprang up and shoved his sleeping bag into a stuff sack; I reached down and began rolling up his ground pad.

"What's this?" I asked as one of Win's postcards covered in loopy handwriting emerged from beneath the pad.

He dropped the sleeping bag and snatched the postcard quickly out of my hand. "Nothing," he said. "For my . . . my uncle. To let him know where we are," he said.

I shook my head. "You need to call him again."

"I will." He crammed the postcard into his handlebar bag. "Let's get out of here, though. Weather's good. Bet we'll hit Minnesota by lunch. Just stay close," he ordered, cramming the last of his gear into his panniers. "You wouldn't want me to wander off like that again, right?" he said, rolling his eyes.

"Shut up and ride," I said, embarrassed a bit at the panic I'd felt, but still wondering if it wasn't justified.

CHAPTER FIFTEEN

"And thus, the coefficient of the variable is indeterminable," my calculus professor said from the front of the room. I wasn't paying attention—even though this had become a favorite class. Not because I was that big of a math geek, but because Dr. Noelle Liston was young, funny, and way more beautiful than a PhD in math had a right to be.

But even her looks couldn't keep me committed to math today. My mind wandered back to the postcard that I'd been carrying around for the last couple days. I reached into the front pocket of my backpack, slid it out, and reread it for the hundredth time. Two days had passed since Mr. Coggans's visit. I hadn't heard from him or Ward.

And as if it weren't enough that I was freaked out about all of this, my anger and jealousy of Win had grown. The muscles I'd discovered over the summer were atrophying as I applied my mind to theoretical physics, while Win was probably riding centuries to drop off a lousy postcard. Once I realized it was from Win, I did so many push-ups and chin-ups in my dorm room that my arms throbbed the next morning. It was a stupid way I tried to punish him, when he didn't even have a chance to compete. But it was all I had. Any relief I'd felt at knowing Abe Ward was wrong was flooded away by the knowledge that Win was still out there riding—*happy*. Meanwhile, I was busting tail at school *and* dealing with his dad.

People around me started to twitch as the class drew to a close. "Don't forget to do the sample problems for Tuesday," Dr. Liston shouted above the din.

I slammed shut a book that easily equaled the weight of all my gear on the bike trip and shoved it into my bag as I headed for the door.

Outside I found a familiar face awaiting me.

"Hey," I said without breaking stride.

"Nice to see you, too, Chris," Ward said as he fell into step beside me. Today he looked like he could be a nontraditional student—dressed casually in jeans and a polo. No gun.

"I've got to go change for work," I said.

"But you don't work on Thursdays," he said, reminding me he had my schedule—my life—in that little notebook I'd seen him jotting things in.

"I switched shifts with a guy. He's taking mine right before Labor Day so I can leave earlier," I said.

"Ah," he muttered.

I shoved open the door. "I'm kind of in a hurry."

"Have you heard from Win?" he asked me. I stopped walking.

"No," I lied, shaking my head and trying to look surprised by the question. The postcard felt like it might burst into flame at any moment. I realized even as I said these words that I was protecting Win for one reason only: habit. "I thought you figured he was, you know, *unreachable*."

He shrugged. "Just a theory. There are other possibilities to consider. Leads to pursue."

"Such as?"

"Well, I'm really not at liberty to say," he said.

I smiled. He had nothing. Which meant Coggans still had nothing. Which still made me happy on some ridiculous level.

"Well, good luck, I guess," I said, resuming my pace back to the dorm.

"I know Coggans came by to see you," he said.

"Yeah, thanks for the warning."

"He isn't going to let this go, Chris," he said, lingering behind me.

"He never lets anything go," I shot back without turning, though I could read the subtext. He'd made that clear two days ago.

"He's convinced you know something. He doesn't like feeling that he's being made a fool of."

"I can't help what he feels," I said, still without slowing.

"Chris, Winston Coggans is in a position to make things financially difficult for your family," he said.

I froze. "What did you just say?"

"He asked me to mention that to you," he said, the regret clear in his voice.

I turned to face him. "He's threatening me?" My face flushed hot. Ward didn't respond, just looked off into the distance.

"This is insane," I said, turning to head up the steps to my dorm. He sighed. "Yeah."

I bolted inside without bothering to answer. Halfway to my room I pulled my cell out of my bag and dialed home. The phone rang in my ear as I cradled it against my shoulder while I unlocked my door. Mom answered on the third ring, just as I chucked my bag on my bed and reached for my kitchen uniform.

"Hey," I said.

"Chris!" She sounded surprised. She had a right to be. I usually waited on my parents to call me. "Any news about Win?"

"Um, no," I hedged, wondering if I should tell her or Dad about the postcard.

"I'm really starting to worry, Chris," she said, though I knew she'd crossed over from worry to panic weeks ago. "Even Win wouldn't go this long with calling," she said. "His poor mother—"

"Mom, has anything changed at work lately?" I asked. I didn't know if I could fake concern for Win's mother now that I knew Win was still out there somewhere.

"Work? No, it's fine—"

"What about Dad?"

"Christopher, do you need money?" I could hear the tinge of alarm in her voice now.

"No, Mom," I said, "I've got plenty." They didn't have it to spare anyway. "What about Dad?"

"Dad's good. Work's good. Are you sure you're all right?"

I breathed for the first time since Ward's implication.

"I'm fine, Mom, really. Forget it," I said.

"Are you sure?"

"Yeah. So nothing's new at work?" I asked again.

"Not really. Well, George sold Mencken's, but I don't see how that's big news," she said.

"What?" Mencken's was my father's construction company.

"I know, weird, isn't it? The business has been doing so well, and George was talking about apprenticing someone to your father to have him start doing more bids—"

"Who bought it, Mom?" I asked, tugging on the grimy running shoes I wore in the kitchen.

"I'm not sure . . . somebody corporate. Your dad can tell you."

That wasn't too alarming. Dad had told me once that bigger companies approached Mr. Mencken all the time, but he was never ready to sell. Dad got offers from those same outfits, but he'd been working for George so long he'd earned his pick of jobs.

"Must have been a sweet deal," was all I managed to say.

She paused. "Are you sure you're all right?"

"Fine," I said. "But I've got to get to work."

"Classes okay?"

"Fine, Mom. I've really got to go," I said.

"Is that agent still hanging around?"

"No," I said quickly. I was afraid if I talked with her any longer, she'd manage to drag the truth out of me. "Mom, I'm going to be late—"

"Wait a second. You got some more mail today—actually, it's

been piling up for a while. Do you want me to send it, or do you think you want us to come get you for Labor Day weekend?"

The holiday weekend was barely enough time to get back and forth to West Virginia. I knew Mom would drive down to pick me up if I asked, but it hardly seemed worth it. I still hadn't let her know what I wanted to do. "What kind of mail?" I asked, rummaging on my dresser for my name tag.

"A cycling magazine, a few postcards, another one from that weird girl. The one with the awful handwriting you had that special time with," she said. "Do you want to come home for break, Chris? We really don't mind the drive."

"You're reading them?" I shouted, ignoring her plea.

"Chris, they're postcards. Nobody expects that the message will be private when they send them. This Tricksey's the only one who's written twice. You must have made quite an impression on her." I could hear the smile in my mother's voice.

"Send it, Mom. As soon as you can," I said.

"Well"—she sounded surprised—"apparently she made quite an impression on you, too. I'll send it all Priority tomorrow."

"Thanks. I've really got to go," I said.

"All right, honey. Love—"

I punched the end-call button on the phone before she finished. But instead of rushing out the door and down campus to work, I sank back on my bed and stared at the ceiling. The second postcard meant that Win was definitely still alive, and maybe even staying put. Nothing was really clear, but everything pointed to one irrefutable fact.

I had to find Win.

CHAPTER SIXTEEN

"Let's eat," I said as we pedaled through a flat stretch of Montana, the seventh week of our ride.

"Anything on the map?" Win shouted from behind me.

I shook my head. "Not much. That was the last biggish town for a while we just passed. Looks like there's a little place called Virden about two miles up."

"We don't have any food," he said.

"Yeah, we do."

"No way. We haven't bought groceries in, like, two days."

I sighed. "Actually, *you* haven't bought groceries in two weeks. But the stuff we bought Wednesday is holding out."

"What, are you growing food in your panniers now?"

"I can't even grow a beard. We've still got everything because we crashed that T-ball team picnic yesterday, and you decided we had to get pizza last night," I said.

"Ah . . . the all-you-can-eat buffet," he said dreamily.

I ignored him. "So, short of a wedding reception we can invite ourselves to, I think we're on our own today. Let's eat anyplace that will give us water."

"How much do you think we ate last night? I think I had at least two whole pizzas," he said.

"Win? Water?"

"Whatever."

A few minutes later we reached Virden. The dot on the map was actually a lot more impressive than the town itself. A few run-down buildings clustered together around a church and a general store that looked to have been closed since the Nixon administration.

"I hear this place gets crazy on the weekends," I said.

"Clubs," Win deadpanned as we rode through the nothing town. We stayed on Route 2 and passed the last house three minutes after entering, without seeing so much as a park bench.

"That wasn't a town!" Win cried. "How did that ruin get a whole dot on the map? We've gotta call AAA."

"Is that a rest stop?" I asked, pointing thirty yards up to the right of our lane.

"Think so. And a welcome oasis it is after bustling Virden," he said.

We steered our bikes off the road and into the parking lot. There were no cars—it seemed as deserted as the town we'd just left. At the center of the compound, atop a knoll of Day-Glo green grass, stood a small picnic shelter. It was flanked on either side by a pair of toilets. In front stood a stone water fountain, complete with a spigot for filling larger containers. Across the small parking lot was a tiny brick building — about the size of a garden shed. A sign above the only window identified it as the U.S. post office for Virden, Montana.

"This'll do," I said, swinging my leg over the back of my bike and stepping off before I'd even braked to a full stop.

Within minutes we had our lunch spread out on the splintered wooden table. I was cutting off slabs of cheddar and arranging them on my onion bagel with a layer of salsa. Win licked his fingers as a mixture of peanut butter, jam, granola, and honey oozed from a stuffed flour tortilla.

"Chips?" he asked me between mouthfuls.

"Over there," I said, gesturing with my pocketknife toward a bag half buried under the bagels.

Win grabbed it with his free hand, put one corner in his teeth, and pulled.

"Dude, wait. . . ."

But it was too late. The bag exploded, showering the tabletop and concrete pad, surrounding us in generic Ruffles.

Win smiled. "I hate reaching into the bag anyway."

I shot him a look.

"What?" he said. "Gets my arm all greasy." He dropped the sack and scooped up a handful of chips from the middle of the table. "Mmm . . . extra crunchy."

I shrugged, topped off my bagel, and snatched a chip. Win rose and ambled around the small rest area, clutching the burrito in his balled fist. At the edge of the maintained area a line of brush formed a natural fencerow, separating us from a farmer's field.

He swallowed, wandered back to the table for more chips, but stooped just inside the shelter to eat a few that had fallen there. "Feels big out here, you know?"

I looked around. All I saw were the two bathrooms, this shelter, and the tiny post office. It seemed dwarfed by its open surroundings. "Yeah, huge."

He smiled. "Not this. Not Virden. *Here.*"

I looked a little beyond, where the sky seemed so deep and empty it almost hurt to look at it. The crops stretched out in all directions, hemmed in to the west by the giant, craggy peaks of the Rockies.

Win was right—it was huge.

"A guy could do some thinking in space this big," Win said, almost whispering.

"And manage to keep in touch," I said, nodding toward the post office.

I grabbed a handful of chips and stood, crossed the empty parking spaces to the brick building. Win followed.

"What's a post office doing out here in the middle of nowhere at a rest stop, anyway?" I asked.

Win shrugged. We studied the hand-painted sign on the drawn shade. "Closed, too. Only open Monday through Thursday."

"Are post offices allowed to be closed?" I asked between bites.

"Virden makes its own rules," Win said.

We ate in silence for a few seconds, studying the building.

"You know what this is?" Win said. "It's like some place that Unabomber guy would have come to send his mail."

I stared at him.

"C'mon. You know what I'm talking about. Out here, in the middle of nowhere, he could drive up late at night and toss something in that slot," he said, pointing toward a letter drop in the front door. "Then he just drives away. Nobody would ever know who sent it. And he could be anywhere within a hundred miles of here. You'd never find him."

"Maybe you shouldn't have quit therapy," I said, returning to the table for my water bottle.

"I'm just saying a guy can sort of get lost out here," he said.

I grabbed both bottles and crossed to the tap in front of the shelter. "Good thing we've got a map, then," I said as I uncapped the bottles and turned on the water.

Win popped the tail of his burrito into his mouth and shrugged. "Never mind."

"You done?" I asked, switching the bottles under the tap. "We've got an easy afternoon, but there's not much for another fifty miles or so. If the dots on the map turn out to be anything like Virden here, we could be in trouble."

He didn't respond.

"So fill up your water now, just in case."

Still he said nothing.

"Win?"

My friend crossed his arms and looked around one last time. I turned off the water and returned to the table, where I began cleaning up our mess and shoving food back into our panniers.

"Win?" I repeated. "Give me a hand?"

He nodded. "Yeah, okay. Virden's getting kind of old already anyway."

CHAPTER SEVENTEEN

"'Water, water, everywhere, Nor any drop to drink' . . . what the heck does that mean, anyway? Chris? Chris, are you listening?"

"Sorry?" I said, turning to Vanti.

"Chris, this is important. We need to do well on this assignment. And we need to figure out what the heck this Coleridge guy is trying to say," she said.

"Water, right. He's saying something about a lot of water," I said.

She stared at me.

"But they can't drink it," I sputtered.

She rolled her eyes. "You suck."

"What?" I said.

She sighed and held out her hand. "Give it."

"Give what?"

"The postcard you've been sneaking looks at for the past half hour."

I shrugged. "It's sort of personal."

"Personal? So are my GPA, my academic eligibility, and my future. If that postcard's so important, then the least you can do is tell me why I'm sacrificing those things so you can sit here and be distracted."

I sighed. "Sorry. I'll focus."

She stared at me some more. Ward should be taking lessons from this girl. Granted, I liked staring at her.

"Okay," I reached into my book for the postcard, and slid it across the table. "Here."

She raised it to eye level, leaving me to stare at the picture on the reverse—a photo of a potato stamped with an outline of the state of Idaho, superimposed above the words THIS SPUD'S FOR YOU.

Vanti read in a voice befitting the library. "'Hey, Chris. Hope things are okay there. Wondering why I haven't heard from you yet. The sky seems bigger every morning, and I actually saw the northern lights for the first time last week. Your friend, Tricksey H.'" I looked around as she read. I don't know if it was my imagination or if Ward's constant presence had me paranoid, but I was pretty sure that the guy sitting with his back to us in the study carrel twenty feet away was the same one I'd seen on a bench outside the sciences building yesterday when I left physics.

It was the jacket that tipped me off. This green leather number with something on the shoulder—what were they, dice? Not that a guy with questionable fashion sense hanging around campus and then studying at the library was cause for alarm. But this guy had to be at least thirty-five. By itself, that wasn't that unusual. There were plenty of nontrads and a few eighth-year seniors on campus. But this guy never carried a bag or a book. Which either explained his lack of timely matriculation or my paranoia. Fact was, if he wanted to, I'm pretty sure Coggans could get the reference librarian to try and take me out.

Vanti lowered the postcard. "Are you kidding me? That's the most impersonal thing I've ever read. I've read juicier stuff in the student handbook."

"There's some good stuff in there—," I began.

"Chris!"

"Sorry."

"So you're obsessing over the most boring postcard ever from some *Lord of the Rings* freak instead of studying with me? You sure know how to make a girl feel special," she said.

"You know Tolkien?" I asked, surprised at this new reason to worship her.

She rolled her eyes. "This is an engineering school, for God's sake. Of course I know Tolkien. It's like an admission requirement. But stop trying to change the subject."

"It's kind of hard to explain," I said.

"Try. Tell me all about your pen pal in"—she squinted at the postmark—"in . . . what's this word—Virgin? Virgin, Montana. They can't name a town that, can they?"

"Shh!"

She stared at me. "You shushed me!" she said.

I grabbed the card, took a peek at Jacketman. He hadn't stirred. "This is the library," I said.

"Chris, you're acting weird. Spill."

"What do you want to know?"

"Male or female?"

The question caught me off guard. Did that mean she was jealous?

"It's complicated," I said. I'd told her a little bit about Win and the investigation when she asked again about the trip one day after class. If I gave her a few minutes more, she'd figure it out on her own. She'd picked up the Hobbit reference in no time. I'd taken nearly a day to grab that one, though to be fair, this time Win had added the *H* for insurance.

I started to speak, thought I saw a stir of green leather, and grabbed a scrap of paper. I wrote quickly. *Male. Win.*

Her mouth dropped open. "But I thought . . ."

I shook my head and pointed at the paper.

She rolled her eyes and grabbed a pen. *How do you know?*

Just do. Shouldn't tell you anything else.

She huffed, scribbled furiously. *Did you tell the FBI guy yet?*

I read as she wrote, shook my head no.

Anybody? she added to the note.

I pointed at her.

"Jeez," she said, lapsing out of note-writing mode as she sank back in her chair. "What are you going to do?"

"Figure out what the heck Coleridge is talking about," I said.

"I mean about—," she began.

"I know what you meant. Maybe go out there."

"Chris, this is serious. You should tell somebody," she whispered.

"I just did."

She smirked. "Besides me."

I grabbed the paper and wrote. *Tell them what? Two postcards from the same place? Win could still be anywhere.*

She stared at me for a long moment, then wrote, *Do you want to find him?*

I sighed, whispered, "I don't know. On the one hand, I think if I do, all this will stop and my life will be normal again. On the other . . . I don't know, Vanti."

The little alarm on her watch began to beep. She snapped to attention. "Crap. I have practice."

"And I've got several hours of indecisive postcard staring ahead of me," I said.

"We'll talk about this later, though?"

I shrugged.

We walked out together, the late-afternoon sun still warm and bright in the August air.

"Hey, Collins," I heard that familiar voice say.

"Please, God, no," I said under my breath.

"Aren't you going to introduce me to your friend?" Ward called out, gesturing toward Vanti.

"I'm Avantika," she said. "And I'm also late for soccer." She turned to me. "Call me later, okay?"

I nodded, and both Ward and I watched her go.

"You must be doing something right," Ward said. I didn't

bother asking him how he'd found me. I'd quit being surprised at his ability to track me down on a campus of 25,000 students.

"What is it today?" I said. "Threats? Allegations?"

"Just wanted to check in," he said.

"You fought rush-hour traffic to say hi?"

"Coggans is getting impatient, Chris. He won't be able to stall Dartmouth much longer. Win's going to lose his spot."

I said nothing.

"I'm sort of running into a wall here," he said. "I've got a case-load that I've been neglecting to work on this thing."

Still I said nothing.

"Anything else you can give me to move this thing along? 'Cause if you can't, I might have to tell Win's dad I'm writing it off."

I didn't believe that for a second.

"I can't help you," I said.

He nodded. "Then, I guess I'm about done here. I might have a few papers for you to sign next week. Will you be around?"

I played along with his bluff. "Labor Day. Long weekend. Even longer since they're upgrading the networks. No classes Thursday or Friday either. What do you want signed, anyway? I thought this was all sort of unofficial."

"Heading home, then?" he asked, ignoring my question.

We had reached my dorm, and I had the handle of the door in my hand. "Probably," I said.

He stared at me. Again, not nearly as intoxicating as when Avantika did so. "What are you going to do, Chris?" he asked. Something in his tone told me he didn't just wonder about my plans for break.

"Just send whatever you want signed to my address here," I said. "And have fun with Win's dad."

He put his hands in his pockets and watched me disappear inside the building. I knew that wasn't the last I'd see of Abe Ward.

When I got back to my room, Jati was eating tuna fish straight from the can and watching pro wrestling on TV. He didn't acknowledge me as my cell phone began buzzing in my pocket.

My father's number flashed beneath the words "incoming call" on the phone's tiny screen.

"Dad?" I said, answering and slipping back into the hallway.

"Chris," my father said. "And your mom says you never pick up."

"She calls when I'm in class," I said.

"We need to talk," my dad said. "I don't want to worry your mother, so if we could just keep this between us—"

"Dad, what's going on?"

He sighed. "Winston Coggans came to see me today. Out at the job."

"Coggans came out there?" I tried to picture Win's dad in one of his expensive suits amid the dirt and machinery of one of my dad's sites. It didn't fit.

"Says he's worried about Win. Wanted to know if we knew anything. Wanted to know if you'd heard from him," he said.

I wondered what it would mean to tell my father about the postcards. What advice he might have for me. But I couldn't make him responsible. "Did he stick around long?"

"Maybe half an hour." My father paused. "Long enough to make sure we all knew he's the one who bought George out."

My stomach jumped. "He what?"

"Yeah," my dad said, "Titan's the new owner. With George retiring, Coggans made it clear he'd need someone to run things."

"He offered you a raise?" I said, confused. This didn't sound like Win's dad putting the hurt on my family's cash flow.

"Not exactly. I think he called it an exchange."

"Exchange?"

"Yeah. In his mind it's a good deal. He seems to think you can produce Win. That unless you do, well, something might happen."

"Something?" I asked.

"Yeah. That's the thing with Coggans. He never came out and said anything. It was like talking to the wind. Things kept changing direction so fast that I'm still not sure if I got fired or promoted."

"Dad. I'm sorry."

"Doesn't seem like you've got anything to be sorry about, Chris."

But I sort of did.

"Did you tell him anything, Dad?"

He laughed. "Told him I didn't know anything to tell. Told him *my son* makes his own decisions."

I hesitated. If I told him, he'd have to lie if Win's dad asked again. He'd have to lie to Mom.

"You know something, Chris?" It wasn't a question.

"Maybe," I said.

"The postcards?"

"How did you—"

"Your mother. She thought it was cute or something that you'd been getting those cards. Showed the second one to me. I thought it sounded strange. Sounded like . . ."

"Like Win?" I offered.

"A bit," he said.

"Did you tell Win's dad about them?" I asked.

"No."

"Did he say anything else?"

"Not really. But he spent quite a bit of time with George, looking over financial statements, asking about the payroll."

My heart sank deeper.

"Dad, I—"

"Listen, Chris. Win's father will do what he's going to do. I need you to do what you think you should—nothing more."

"But your job—"

"Will be fine," he said, "one way or another."

"I can't let him do this."

"Let me worry about Coggans. I trust you to do what's right here."

I couldn't reply. My dad loved me. He loved his job. But he also loved Win.

"What are you going to do, Chris?" he asked. I realized that was the third time in an hour I'd been asked that question.

"I don't think I'm coming home for the weekend, Dad."

"And I have a feeling I don't want to know where you're going," he said. "What should I tell your mom?"

"Tell anybody who asks that I'm going backpacking on a section of the Appalachian Trail with some guys from my floor."

"Got it," he said.

"Are you sure about this?" I asked him.

"Absolutely. Do the right thing," he repeated.

"That'd be easy if I knew what it was," I said.

"You'll know."

"At least I know where to start looking," I said.

CHAPTER EIGHTEEN

Fifty miles turned out to be a lot harder than we'd anticipated. The wind kicked up that afternoon, swirling dust around our faces. My mouth felt like cotton, and I burned through my water without thinking. The wind crept in around my sunglasses, drying out my eyes. The pain was so bad that I was riding now with my chin tucked to my chest, keeping the white line inches from my front wheel. I'd look up periodically to make sure nothing had appeared in the shoulder in front of us, and then duck back down before my eyes began to tear up again, making it impossible to see.

"This wind is evil," Win shouted, his voice almost carried away before it reached me. The space we'd allowed to stretch out between us over the last few weeks had snapped back, and now Win drafted off me, only a foot or two separating my rear wheel from his front.

"It's just wind," I said. We'd faced headwinds before—the fact that wind sweeps predominantly from west to east across the country was something we learned the hard way. But I'd never felt so beaten by it. "It can't be evil."

It began to blow even harder. We plowed on in silence for another half an hour, crouching low on the handlebars to minimize surface area. My panniers caught enough air to make it seem at times like I was pedaling a stationary bike instead of one that had carried me more than two thousand miles. Even in my lowest gear I fought to keep the bike moving forward, my legs burning, throat crying out for a drink. And we couldn't stop—we had to make it to a town to get water.

And then Win started screaming.

I was so alarmed that I almost tipped over. I managed to unclip a pedal, put a foot down, and half turn in time to see Win jumping off his bike and throwing it to the shoulder of the road.

"Flat?" I asked, though I was pretty sure this wouldn't have elicited such a reaction.

He just kept screaming. Then he tore off his helmet and threw it lamely into the wind. It wasn't heavy to begin with—just some hard foam covered with plastic and a few straps—so it only went forward a few feet before the wind overtook the force of Win's toss and shoved it right back. It nailed him squarely in the chest.

"See! It *is* evil!" he said, as if this event were proof, before he resumed screaming and thrashing at the air.

I said nothing, just dismounted my bike, wheeled it back a few yards, and laid it next to Win's. I took off my own helmet and set it on the ground, then perched myself on top of it. This could take a while.

Win continued to yell. Truth was, I might have freaked out on the wind if he hadn't first, but now that I saw him, so pathetic and futile, I felt numbed. So I just watched and listened and let him get it out of both our systems.

And then Win did something surprising. He started to cry—something I've seen him do only twice in all the years that we've been friends. Both were after his father called him into his study, closed the door, and left me outside to wonder what was going on. I never heard voices raised or the snap of a belt or anything like that. But both times Win emerged barely holding back a flood of tears. The crying waited until he was safely in the backyard, hurling rocks at a tree.

Now he was hurling gravel by the handful at a speed limit sign. "It's trying to push me back!"

It seemed unwise to point out that he had been drafting behind me for the sixteen miles we'd managed since our lunch stop at the phantom post office.

"I'm not going back!" he screamed into the air, sounding like a four-year-old threatening not to go to school.

"The wind'll die down, Win," I said, but he wasn't listening to me.

"I'm going to make it," he shouted again, but with less vehemence.

Then I realized that he wasn't saying "we." *I'm not going back.*

But before I could ask him what he meant, another voice pulled my attention away.

"Nice day, huh?" I turned to find another cyclist braking to a stop as he crossed the road. Since he was riding east, he actually had to brake pretty hard to overcome the force of the wind.

"This wind is murder, isn't it?" he said as he climbed off his bike and took a swig from his water bottle.

We'd met other cyclists on our journey, even ridden with this young couple for a day or two right after we crossed into Minnesota. This guy's appearance was unusual only in the way he'd sort of sneaked up on us. He must have just crested the hill, and since he had the benefit of the tailwind pushing him along at probably thirty-five miles an hour, he was here before I had a chance to notice him. All his gear was brand-new and looked expensive. Instead of saddlebags, he was hauling a two-wheeled trailer attached to the rear fork of his bike. It had a ridiculous caution flag fluttering about seven feet up a reedy pole. In the wind it bent down to brush his helmet.

"I tell you," the stranger shouted, "this wind's enough to make a man crazy." Win ignored him, kept a safe distance, where his tears could not be seen.

"Damn flag keeps knocking into my eyes," he said.

I couldn't think of anything to say to the old fart complaining about a tailwind that had him cruising along in his highest gear.

"You guys got any patches?" he asked. "I ran out back at Glacier."

I pushed up off the pavement. "Yeah, I got a couple you can have," I said, reaching for the zipper on my pannier pocket. I'd just bought a kit yesterday. I fished out two patches and handed them over. "Here."

"Thanks," he said. "Where you boys heading?"

"Seattle," I said. This guy bugged me.

"Just left Seattle myself," he said, adding, "bound for Florida. Been out ten days."

I did some quick mental math. He'd been enjoying tailwinds daily if he'd made that kind of time.

"But this wind," he said again, "this wind's about to make me lose it. It just blows and blows and blows."

"Sort of like some people," I said.

"Say again?" he asked.

"Nothing," I muttered.

"You guys thinking about camping here tonight?" he asked. "'Cause if you are, I might join you. Don't think I feel like going another twenty miles to town with this flag beating on my helmet the whole way," he half laughed.

"Gee," I said, "that really sucks." I could have pointed out that removing the flag might be just crazy enough to work, but that would have been helpful. I'd already fulfilled my road karma with the patch donation.

"Actually, we were just leaving," Win said, snatching up his helmet and righting his bike.

I nodded. "Yeah, no water, no scamp," I said, sounding cheerful.

He seemed to deflate a little at this rejection, looking like he could use a patch job himself. Maybe having someone to listen to him bitch about a tailwind all night would have made his whole day worthwhile. "Nice riding, then," he said, climbing back onto his bike. He turned his wheels into the stream of the wind and caught the air like a sail. He was a quarter mile away in thirty seconds.

"Idiot," Win muttered, jamming his foot into the clip.

I laughed. Glad to have my friend doing more than going postal on a natural phenomenon.

"Complete," I agreed. "Didn't even occur to him to take that flag off."

Win pushed down on his pedal, shouted over his shoulder. "I didn't mean him," he said in a way that made me know he didn't mean me, either.

"Follow me," he said. "Your turn to draft for a while." I obeyed, still a little stunned by the transformation.

Six mile markers and an hour later we saw the truck. Since balancing at such a slow pace was proving impossible, we'd dismounted three times to push our bikes into the wind.

The beat-up Chevy sat parked beside the road, fifty yards or so from where a man in overalls and a trucker hat was peering into the open engine of a red tractor.

Grateful for a little bit of shelter, we hunkered down behind the pickup.

"This is insane," I said, wondering if Win hadn't been right that the wind was less a force of nature and more a form of evil. I still hadn't shaken his comment or asked him about it. *I'm not going back.*

"We're not riding anymore today," he said, leaning his bike against the pickup and walking toward the tractor.

"Where're you going?" I shouted.

He called back over his shoulder without stopping, "To get us out of here."

I followed, caught up to him as he pulled level with the farmer.

"Excuse me, sir?" Win said. The man pulled his head from under the canopy and turned to survey us.

"Afternoon, boys," he said, dropping the wrench into a toolbox at his feet.

"Sir," Win began, his voice hoarse, "we're riding our bikes cross-country, and we've come all the way from West Virginia. But now we've got this wind, and there's no way we'll make it to water tonight on our own."

The man turned, leaning against the giant wheel. He surveyed the way the wheat in the field across the road was bending and thrashing. "Probably not," he agreed.

"So, if it's not too much trouble, could you maybe give us a lift to town? We can throw our bikes in the back. We'll even pay you for gas," he said. I wondered if this might be the time that Win broke into that stash of bills he had hidden in his pannier.

The farmer frowned. "What'd you say your name was, son?"

"Win . . . my name's Winston."

"And you?" he asked, pointing a greasy hand at me.

"Chris," I offered.

He smiled. Looked down at his hands, said more to himself than to us, "That was my boy's name."

I didn't know what to say to that. Neither did Win, so we just looked at each other and waited for the farmer to speak again.

"I don't get up to town much," he said after a long pause. "And

I don't think I'll be heading in tonight. Camp at my farm if you like. There's water, and you can set your tent up in the barn to get out of this wind."

I looked to Win. This was probably the best offer we could hope for. "Okay," Win said.

The farmer nodded. "Name's Morgan." He offered a hand creased black with oil. I took it and was surprised by the strength of his grip. After shaking Win's hand, he lifted his toolbox and headed toward the truck. "That thing's not going to get fixed today," he said, nodding back at the tractor. "Let's go."

He dropped the tailgate, shoved his toolbox shrieking along the beat-up bottom. Win and I lifted our bikes onto the bed and closed the gate.

He climbed into the driver's seat, reached over, and opened the passenger door. "Sticks from the outside," he said as we slid in. I straddled the engine well in the middle, my knees inches from my chin.

Morgan started the engine. "You boys rode those bikes all this way?"

I nodded. "Yes, sir."

"This is the first time we've hitched," Win said.

Morgan seemed to consider this. "Then, I suppose we ought not actually cover any ground," he said.

I was confused, but I understood what he meant as soon as he turned the wheels off the highway shoulder and aimed for the field. In the distance I could see a yellow two-story farmhouse with a porch hugging its front and sides, a grove of tall oaks jerking and swaying in the wind.

"No such thing as a shortcut on any journey worth making," he added.

This guy understood. On a level that he didn't even have to ask about, he got it.

"But the field . . . ," I began as the pickup bounced along the rows, green plants thrashing at the doors.

He shook his head. "Just peas. Ready to harvest anyway. I'll be driving through 'em in a few days when I get that tractor mended."

Win was smiling.

"Ever had fresh peas?" Morgan asked.

I shrugged. "Maybe?"

"If a man don't know if he's had fresh peas, he ain't had fresh peas," he said, opening the truck door without easing off the accelerator. In the next moment he leaned out, swooped an arm down from the cab, and came back up a second later with a handful of broken plants bearing perfect green pods.

"Well, that's hardly going to feed one of us," he said. "Win?"

The smile didn't change as Win threw open his door and repeated the process two or three times, until I was holding a pile of peas and branches on my lap. I laughed. So did Win. Morgan smiled.

"I love the wind," Win said.

This time I knew exactly what he meant.

CHAPTER NINETEEN

"Folks, we're making real good time, so I'm gonna pull the bus on over and have a smoke," the driver mumbled into the speaker. It was two in the morning. I hadn't been able to sleep, but I was pretty sure the driver was using the smoke breaks to stay awake. The bus stopped, and half a dozen people filed out. I stood, stowed my bag on my seat, and headed up the aisle.

I hadn't taken up smoking, but peeing under the stars and getting a little fresh air seemed in order.

I had the postcard—the second one from the Unabomber box that my mother had forwarded—in my pocket. And she'd called right before the long weekend began and told me that another one had arrived, same postmark. Win wanted me to find him.

After all he'd put me through, I wasn't keen to give Win what he wanted. For the last ten years he'd had a knack for getting his way—either by laziness or by manipulation. Now that he was completely screwing up my life, I resented this even more. And it wasn't just mine. My dad's job was in peril.

But here I was, even though I had only a general range of where Win could be. Assuming he was still using his bike, he couldn't be traveling from that far away to mail the cards. Morgan's farm was somewhere between Virden and Browning. With the hills, I figured the maximum he could do in an out-and-back ride was around ninety miles, if he was still in shape.

Even if he was at the farm, I had no idea how to get there. I'd never figured out if Morgan was a first or last name, and I doubted if I could have instructed anybody on how to get to his place just looking at a map. There must have been two dozen farms stretched across that piece of Route 2 on the way to Glacier, all with the same peeling paint, endless fields, and looming mountains.

But he'd be there. And the truth was, I wanted to find him. Partly because I was so pissed. Pissed that I was pretty sure he knew exactly what he was doing—exactly how his folks would react and what a mess he'd made of my life. That part wanted to find him, beat the crap out of him, and then haul his carcass back to his parents and Abe Ward.

But the other part of me was pulled by something less definitive than anger. Maybe it was just the need to see if he was all right. Maybe it was to find out what the hell he'd been thinking when he ditched me. Maybe just to see if he was the same person.

I descended the last step and walked past the huddle of nicotine addicts sharing lighters and stories. I went about thirty yards beyond, where their smoke couldn't pollute the clean, chilled air, and unzipped my fly.

I knew this place. By some freaky, random coincidence, the bus had been forced off the freeway by road construction early last night. Now we were following Route 2, passing spots I remembered from the bike trip.

A few hours ago we'd taken a smoke break half a mile from a trailer where Win and I had stopped for water. Last summer we knocked on the screen door, and three little kids crowded at the mesh as their mother spoke to us from inside. After she pointed out the spigot on the side of the house, the kids cautiously edged out, peeked at our bikes like they were racehorses, and began asking questions. The mother, at first watching us suspiciously from the top stoop, eventually made it all the way to the bottom, where she sat holding her sides and giggling as we told her and her kids a couple of the funnier anecdotes from the trip. She gave us a whole banana cream pie when we left, making us promise not to eat it until we'd had our dinner that night. Win made a show of tying it down carefully across his handlebars, the plastic lid and edges of the aluminum pie tin buckling under the strain of the bungee. We made it about two miles, until we were out of sight, then ducked behind an abandoned gas station and downed the pie faster than I could patch a flat.

And an hour ago I'd seen a billboard advertising the Wonder Hut, a random little museum filled with assorted specimens in jars and bottles. It was sort of a mad scientist's zoo—a collection of taxidermy and jars of formaldehyde filled with two-headed fetal pigs or supposed alien remains. After seeing the signs for two hundred miles before we reached it, we were desperate for something more interesting than roadkill, so we forked over the three-dollar admission fee. I got a kick out of it and kept trying to draw Win into making fun of it with me. But something about those animals pinned up on the wall spooked him. He got quiet and ran through it like it was an obstacle course rather than a museum.

Where I stood now was just like the rest of North Dakota: flat and criminally boring. All the same, I convinced myself that it held some significance. This might have been the spot where we began jousting. On these empty stretches with nothing to see, no hills to climb, no lakes to jump into, we'd started wasting water when we should have been saving it. One afternoon I took off in a sprint ahead of Win. He didn't chase me, didn't even ask what I was doing. When I was about fifty yards ahead, I wheeled my bike around, slid my water bottle from its cage, and held it aloft. Even from that distance I saw the smile break. Without a word he pulled out his own bottle, uncapped the stopper valve with his teeth, and held it high. We both increased our tempo, charging toward each other. When we were close enough to hear each other's chains spinning though the freewheels, we lowered our bottles, aimed, and fired. By the time we had three or four more passes like that, we were soaked. And laughing.

The last thirty-six hours on the bus had been filled with memories like this one. And now I was confused. When I thought about all the trouble he was causing, I wanted to find Win and kick his ass. But when I remembered the epic, hilarious, and transcendent moments of the trip, I wanted to find him, get on a bike, and go for another long ride.

The Greyhound's engine turned over, and I began walking backward, gazing at the stars and the silhouette of the hills for as long as I could before turning. I wasn't the only one trying to make the break last. An overweight woman wearing an "Austin 3:16" T-shirt was making the most of the tail end of her Virginia Slim.

I stepped aside to let her climb on first. While she hoisted herself up that first step, I took one last look around, drinking in the stillness and the quiet and the memory. I remembered camping in the open with Win on nights like this, with the stars so close they almost frightened me.

But not that close. I squinted and looked back down the road behind the bus. A pinprick of red-orange light flared in the black for just a moment. Firefly?

But then I saw it flare again and burn just a little longer, before the ember fell to the pavement and disappeared.

"Let's go, kid," the driver said to me.

I pointed to where I'd seen the light. "But I think there's somebody back there," I said.

The driver shook his head. "Nope. Just did a head count. You're the last one on. Again."

I took another glance back where I'd seen what I was sure now was a cigarette tip burning, and pulled myself up the steps. The driver was right, nobody appeared to be missing. But if that person wasn't on our bus, then . . .

The bus lurched back onto the highway as I fumbled down the aisle to my seat. I was certain I'd seen something. And now I was starting to fear what it meant. Starting to wonder what possible reason somebody might have for pulling over in the middle of nowhere on a lonely highway a quarter mile behind a bus at two in the morning.

I collapsed into my seat, palms sweating and heart racing. If someone was back there for the reasons I feared they might be, I'd know soon enough. I stared out the window into the blackness of the prairie.

One Mississippi.

Two Mississippi.

Three Mississippi.

Four Mississippi.

As I counted five, a wash of light from a pair of low-beam head-lights faintly illuminated the pavement just outside my window.

I was being followed.

CHAPTER TWENTY

"You'll make Glacier tomorrow,"
Morgan said between sips of something that looked more like
motor oil than coffee.

The peas were only the start—but they were as good as
promised. Morgan's wife, Effie, had laid out a spread that
rivaled anything my family put on for any major holiday. The
remnants of half a dozen other fresh vegetables, mashed
potatoes, chicken-fried steak, and enough gravy to have me
feeling like I was in a delicious, calorie-induced coma still
littered the white linen tablecloth. A single wedge of blackberry
cobbler lay oozing in the dish at the center of the table, looking
strangely like a crime-scene photo. Win and I had done most of
the damage.

"Last piece?" Effie offered, reaching for the cobbler dish.

Win and I both held up our hands in a *Thanks, but no thanks* gesture.

"For the first time in two months I'm full," he said.

"I was full before the cobbler came, but it was too good to pass up," I said.

"Yeah, somebody's going to have to cut these shorts off me," Win joked.

"Dude. No," I said.

"Joking . . . jeez," he said. Morgan smiled. Effie sighed.

"Our Chris used to pick the berries, just to talk me into making his favorite dessert," she said, smiling sadly.

And that's how the evening had gone. Win and I would be funny, but then, "Our Chris . . ." Our hosts wanted stories, which we tried to be as generous with as the food they heaped on our plates. When they talked about themselves, though, a curtain seemed to fall on their faces. The laughter had been punctuated by heavy, brief silences.

I've had more than I can handle, since Chris isn't here to help.

Our Chris was a good boy—only a couple years older than you two.

Seeing how much it obviously hurt them even to mention the boy who had been their son, the one who filled all the picture frames lining the wall of the hallway, neither Win nor I asked anything about him.

"Well," Morgan broke the silence at last, "you're gonna have a long day, and I've got that tractor . . . ," he trailed off.

He rose from the table. "I'll show you boys the barn and where the water is."

Win and I grabbed plates and bowls and began ferrying them from the screened-in eating porch back into the kitchen through a small window designed for the purpose.

"I'll take care of these, boys," Effie scolded. "Just make sure you're in time for breakfast. Six, okay?"

We both nodded. We hadn't been up before eight in two months, but something told me there'd be more gravy and possibly something else fried.

We followed Morgan out to the barn, retrieving our bikes from where we'd leaned them against the clothesline when we arrived. The wind had fallen away to a steady breeze—but the air tasted faintly metallic and a flash of lightning split the distant sky.

"Storm's coming," Morgan announced.

Win and I just nodded. Now I could feel the tingle in the air, the low current of thunder that boomed the preamble to more.

"Guess that's what that wind was working up all day," Morgan said. "But it'll be clear tomorrow."

We wheeled our bikes the hundred yards to the barn. "She leans," he explained as we reached the giant wooden doors, "but she's dry."

He threw open the door and disappeared into the darkness, and a moment later we were flooded by electric light. Moths fluttered around the bare bulbs, a few breaking orbit to crash into the glow.

"Usually keep the tractor in here," he said, "but we all know that story."

"Cool," I said. And it was. Hay and duff littered the barn floor, promising a soft night's sleep. The breeze blew just enough through the chinks in the siding to keep the air from going stale.

"Loft's up there." He pointed to a ladder along the western wall that disappeared through a hole in the floor above. "But you probably want to sleep down here instead of lugging all your gear up there."

"I don't know," Win said. "Always liked a top bunk myself."

Morgan laughed. "So did my boy. He and his friends used to sleep over up there."

Again that uncomfortable silence seeped in.

"Well, I'll leave you to it. There's fresh water and an outdoor shower on the back of the barn outside."

"There's a shower back there?"

"Yep. Effie makes me use it before I come inside if I'm extra grimy," he said, smiling. "No toilet, though. You can come up to the house and use it, or just cat-hole in those trees east of here," he said, turning for the door.

"Thanks, Morgan," I said. "This is really great."

"Not at all, fellas. Glad to have you," he said, sounding again as sad as a man pretending to smile could be.

He walked off, his boots crunching on the pea-gravel path.

"Very cool," Win said, climbing the ladder to the loft. The wind gusted stronger now, setting the barn creaking at irregular intervals. The thunder drew close. But it was dry and still inside, and the aroma of engine oil and horse tack was comforting. I was feeling so relaxed after that meal and upon finding such a nice place to crash that I was surprised when the faint itching in my legs began.

Win scaled the ladder and poked his head into the loft. "Nice place to sleep, even without the tent up. Save time in the morning," he said. "The other Chris had the right idea."

"What do you think happened to him?"

Win descended. "Dead, I guess. Figure Morgan would have told us if he wanted to. Probably better not to ask," he said.

I shrugged and went over to my bike, tossing my sleeping bag to the ground and digging into my pannier for my wash kit. The first flash of lightning close by cast crazy shadows on the barn walls. The itching in my legs grew stronger with each passing second, but every other part of my body cried out for a warm shower and a long sleep.

"Shotgun on shower," I said. "Wait, is it dangerous to shower in a lightning storm, or is that another one of those things my mom made up?" When Win didn't respond or try to usurp my claim, I turned to face him and understood what my legs had been foretelling.

He was standing in the middle of the straw floor, tools and equipment hanging all over the walls in a way that certain trendy restaurants try very hard to duplicate. The overhead lights hummed.

"In this space," he intoned, "a champion will be crowned." As if on cue, thunder pealed closer than it had before, rattling the equipment hanging on the walls.

I sighed. "I'm not competing for first shower. I called it."

He stared at me, smiling this strange, sad smile. "This isn't about a shower."

"Win, I'm wiped. It was a long day. We've got an early start tomorrow." Still he didn't respond. Just stared and smiled. My legs hadn't quieted down at all.

I tossed my wash kit to the ground next to my bike.

"Fine. What'll it be? Push-up contest again? Arm wrestling?"

"Nope." He crouched into a wrestling stance. "Pin for a three count."

I shook my head. "No way," I said as I picked up my kit and headed for the door.

I heard three quick steps approaching me from behind, but before I could turn around, Win tackled me.

The wash kit flew from my hand and out the open barn doors into the gravel and the coming rain. My footing slipped away from me, and for a moment I was sure Win's sneak attack would prove all the advantage he needed to end this quickly. I scrambled, trying to twist to grab him, and managed to spin him around with his own momentum as we both fell to the ground. In that moment I forgot how tired I was, how sore I was, how full my belly was. I forgot how badly I wanted a shower. All I knew was that I wanted to wrestle.

And I wanted to beat him.

Somehow, from the first moment he hit me, I knew this was different from all the other little contests. Those had just been for bragging rights. But now I didn't just want to win, I wanted to *defeat* Win. Friendly rivalry had been left behind on the road, or maybe this desire was something I'd had all along and just ignored. This time I was fighting to learn who was actually stronger—the better man.

And I was willing to risk losing to find out who that was.

By now we were on our feet, deadlocked, heads down, chests heaving, waiting for an opening. The rain began to fall in great drops, like the sky had been holding back, until the clouds were so heavy they just couldn't hold on any longer. Sheets of water cascaded down on the corrugated metal of the barn roof. I drowned in the sheer noise. It sounded like a crowd had gathered to watch this battle between us.

That's when we started to break apart, I think. Or at least the last link between us began to fail. Because I managed to duck down, grab his right knee, and yank it up sharply. He grasped for my head and arms as I half lifted him in the air, his left foot scrambling for leverage as I drove him back quickly. He shoved me and we separated as the force sent him sailing. I saw my friend flail backward in slow motion and land heavily on the barn floor as lightning split the sky. He quickly popped back onto his feet, the look in his eyes one I hadn't seen from him in years. Surprise.

I was surprised too. Surprised at my own strength. At my confidence. At the fact that I knew I could do this.

We circled each other. As I looked for an advantage, Win dove at me sideways. The strength of his grip on my ankle shocked me and sent me crashing forward to the duff.

We both knew we could pin the other. We both could.

I don't know how long we went on like that. Takedown, reversal, grapple, near pin, escape, repeat. I don't know how many times he threw me, or I threw him. I don't know how his eyebrow split open or how I ripped my elbow, but at one point I lost my hold on Win in the blood and sweat. Part of me was sure we'd go on like this forever—like I'd always expected our friendship would.

Despite the pain and exhaustion in my body, my mind was clear. I knew almost nothing the entire time except one thing: pin him.

That's why I was so surprised when another thought entered my brain. It was like one of those moths banging into the lightbulb overhead, only finally, somehow, it got through.

Jacob wrestling with the angel. Jacob the deceiver. All at once the first night of the trip, scamping at the church, the story the preacher told, flooded back in on me. In that second I knew the story better than I had when I was sitting there in that church. I knew what Jacob had been up to. All the lies he'd told, the ways he'd been escaping, what he'd had to escape from. I knew because that story was playing itself out again. Right here.

I couldn't feel the pain from the bruises I was sure to have tomorrow, or the gash in my elbow, or even the suffocating hold Win had on me. Maybe because something else hurt more. Something else had broken. Damn it. All I know is I could feel the tears beginning to burn at the backs of my eyes.

And I did what most guys do when they're about to cry.

I got really, really pissed.

I don't know how, but a second later I wrenched my body free from a half nelson, spun around, and had Win in a cradle lock with one shoulder planted on the barn floor.

This time he didn't break the hold.

I ground him into the floor, edging the other shoulder down, that preacher's words echoing in my head. *Jacob had to wrestle with that angel! And he was changed!* I could barely breathe. The walls of the barn seemed to close in around me as I bore down.

Finally Win spoke faintly. "Let me go, Chris."

"Giving in?" I asked through clenched teeth, though I knew that wasn't what he meant.

"That's not what I said!" he gasped. *"Let me go."*

Then I remembered how that story ended. Jacob let the angel go. But it felt all mixed up in our version somehow.

It didn't matter. In that second—with those words—Win beat me. I felt as helpless as if he'd pinned me.

Let me go.

I held on for a second longer, a little too long, but then I did what he'd asked.

My body unwound like a coiled spring and I lay back on the ground.

Win sat up, rubbing his neck, and panted, "You've been . . . a good friend . . . Christopher Collins."

I pushed myself to my feet, exhaustion returning as the adrenaline ebbed. The barn was still shrinking. Win's words took up too much room in the tightening space. Air. I needed air.

The rain was slackening off a bit, the thunder now so far away that it surprised me. I stood in the warm rain a moment before I scooped up my water bottle and wash kit. I couldn't look at Win.

"I mean it, Chris. You've been a true friend," Win shouted as I disappeared around the side of the barn, trying to remember if it was Jacob or the angel who'd given the blessing in the story.

CHAPTER TWENTY-ONE

"Hungry Horse, Montana, folks," the driver called out as he threw open the door, I blinked back the sunlight pouring through the oversize windows.

Damn! I pounded my temple on the glass window next to my seat. I'd spent all of yesterday trying to sleep and couldn't, but the few hours I needed to stay awake and wait for my stop, my eyes wouldn't stay open.

I'd slept past the rest area with the mailbox, though that wouldn't have been much help. Slept through the sunrise over Glacier. I'd overshot the farm by at least fifty miles. I was screwed.

The bus driver—a new one (guess I slept through that switch, too)—continued. "This is our breakfast stop, folks. We'll take forty-five minutes. Don't miss the hash brown casserole," he said to us. Man, there were some loud yawners on this bus.

Win and I had stopped here. Eaten about five plates of french fries, even though we'd paid for only one. The waitress—what was her name?—had liked us. She was only a year younger and kept sneaking into the kitchen to refill our plate. She was also a babe.

"What day is it?" I asked the guy across the aisle as I slipped into my Tevas.

"Saturday," he mumbled.

I nodded. I'd been on the bus for two days. A hot meal sounded perfect—if I could afford it. I was short of cash, so I'd used the emergency credit card my parents had cosigned to buy my ticket. With Dad's job in trouble, I figured this had to count as an emergency. I just hoped Mom wouldn't pay too much attention to the "Greyhound Lines" on the statement. If Ward or anybody else was able to check it and see, I just hoped they'd fall for the fact that I'd purchased a ticket for Omak, Washington, five hundred miles farther than where I thought I'd find Win.

I pulled out my wallet and flipped it open, thumbed through the bills. Forty-eight bucks. I had to make this money last for who knew how long, or risk using the card again and giving Ward another way to find out exactly where I'd been.

I waited until the aisle cleared before standing and walking out. Halfway up I stopped. A gray sedan pulled into a parking space by the front door of the restaurant, fifty feet from where the bus sat. A balding man with a potbelly climbed out of the car and stretched his legs. He took a long drag on his cigarette and tossed the butt to the ground, crushing it with the heel of a black cowboy boot.

The man glanced a little too long at the bus and the line of passengers migrating into the diner. And then he reached across the seat, pulled out a dark green leather jacket, and slipped it on.

A dark green leather jacket with a pair of dice embroidered on the shoulder. The same ugly jacket from the library.

Oh, crap.

I sank down into the seat I'd been standing next to. Jacketman continued to keep an eye on the passengers streaming from the bus as he locked his car and walked slowly toward the door. Instead of trying to merge into the crowd, he held the door open and studied each face that entered the diner.

"Gotta lock it up, son," a voice said. I jumped and turned to face the driver, who stared at me impatiently from the front of the bus.

"Right," I mumbled as I stood, keeping my eyes fixed on Jacketman as he gave one last look at the bus and entered the restaurant.

By the time I got into the diner portion of the gas station/diner/gift shop/grocery store, all the tables were already taken. Silverware scraped against plates, conversation like a current in the greasy air.

I scanned the room and saw Jacketman at one end of the counter, perched on a barstool with a clear view of the front door. I took a seat at the opposite end of the counter, a few seats down from where Win and I had sat the last time I was here. Jacketman pretended not to look at me.

I felt like I was going to throw up. My legs wouldn't quit buzzing. And I was starving.

"Coffee?"

I checked the name tag. Danielle. The babe.

She stopped midpour. "Chris! Win said . . ."

That one unguarded phrase told me almost everything I needed to know. But I was more concerned about who else might be listening. I glanced nervously at the other end of the counter. The guy didn't appear to have heard us.

"You remember me?" I asked her. She was still gorgeous. Long blond hair pulled into a braid that started at the base of her neck and trailed halfway down her back, big green eyes. Even in a dorky diner uniform her legs were amazing.

She nodded. "Uh, *yeah*. Nearly got fired over all the fries I gave you two." She laughed. "I'm just surprised, is all," she said, though she sounded cautious. "Win didn't mention you'd be visiting."

"You've seen him?"

"Honey, are you going to take my order, or do I have to turn myself eighteen again for you to notice me?" asked the bus driver from two stools down. He hadn't even bothered to ask for a menu.

Danielle rolled her eyes, finished pouring my coffee. "Hang on," she said, placing the pot back on the warmer and pulling a notepad from her apron pocket.

I watched her. She was another of those girls I'd never have had the guts to talk to before we did the ride. Win and I had argued about who'd seen her first, both of us acting like we could claim her. We were both smitten.

"Three-egg Denver omelet, side of bacon *and* sausage, hash brown casserole, half order of biscuits and gravy?" she confirmed, looking over the top of her notepad.

The bus driver nodded. "Yep."

"Want the bypass surgery with the food, or after, like a chaser?" she asked.

He sighed. "Just keep the coffee coming."

I smiled. Danielle tacked the order to a metal carousel with a magnet, spun it around, and rang a bell. "Order in," she called.

"And what about you?" she turned and asked me.

"I'll have the special," I said loudly, adding in an undertone, "And anything you can tell me about Win."

"Ooh, very slick, with the whispering and all . . ." Her smile faded as she read my gaze. I cut my eyes to the end of the counter. She seemed to understand. Her face shifted slightly. "Special it is," she said, jotting a note on her pad. "I can't help you with Win, though. I'm not actually sure where he's staying. Won't tell me," she added in a whisper.

"He won't tell you?" I asked.

She turned to hang the slip on the carousel. "Changes the subject every time I ask."

Win knew people would be looking for him. Not telling Danielle where he was staying was his way of protecting her and covering his trail. "But you've seen him?"

She nodded. "He comes in on his bike, only without all that gear he had before."

He wouldn't need full gear for a fifty-mile ride, but I suspected he was probably hitching at least part of the way back. Riding a hundred miles in a day wouldn't leave him much time to hang out.

"When did you see him last?"

"Yeah, Glacier is really nice this time of year," she said, "though most people think you have to go up to Maine or something to see the leaves change."

What?

But then I felt a presence at my elbow. Jacketman was pretending to look through the pile of old newspapers on the counter next to me.

"Yeah," I mumbled to Danielle as she sidled down to take another order.

Jacketman lingered a bit longer, finally took the sports page, and returned to his seat. Danielle moved back in my direction, refilling cups of coffee.

"Close one," she said.

"Yeah," I muttered. "Thanks."

When she was satisfied that he wasn't watching, she replaced the coffeepot and picked up a rag to wipe a spot on the counter in front of me that was perfectly clean. "I saw him last weekend," she said, adding, "Like always."

"Like always?" I repeated quietly.

She nodded. "He comes in every Sunday. I work the lunch shift, when it's pretty dead. Nobody wants Sunday dinner in this dive . . . except him."

Every Sunday. Win was making the trip from the farm—if that's where he was—every Sunday to see this girl. I wondered if she knew how far he was riding.

"He's had nearly everything on the menu by now," she said, laughing.

"He's okay?" I asked.

She shrugged. "Yeah. Seems like he did this summer when you two were here together. He's taking me to the Leaf Ball at school next month," she said, watching for my reaction. "It's totally lame, I know, but I'm on the court and needed a date, and he promised he'd let me drive and not try to take me there on the handlebars of his bike, so . . ."

Win had a girlfriend. Win had never had a girlfriend ever, and I never believed either of us would have one as beautiful as Danielle. It added insult to injury in the worst way. Part of me wondered if I'd stuck around, would she have picked me over him?

"Did he tell you anything about what he's doing here?" I asked.

She shook her head. "Not really. Just said he liked it here and decided to stick around for a while. He mentioned he'd found work and a place to stay."

"He say where he's working?" I asked.

She shook her head. "No." She grabbed the coffeepot and began making her rounds again.

When she came back, she refilled mine, pouring slowly. "What are you doing here, Chris? If you didn't know Win was still here . . ."

I took a sip of the coffee. "I'm looking for him," I admitted.

She nodded. "Nobody knows he's here, do they?" she asked quietly.

"Maybe," I said.

"Who else?" she asked, cutting her eyes over to the newspaper Jacketman was hiding behind.

"I think he's FBI," I said. "There's been a different guy asking me questions. Some guy Win's dad has in his pocket."

She shook her head and looked away. Neither of us said anything for a long minute. Apparently they'd been talking about more than school dances and bike rides. The bell rang behind her, and she spun around to pick up two plates, the bus driver's and mine.

"Here you go," she said automatically. "Ketchup?" she asked the driver.

"Salsa, if you got it," the driver said as she bent below the counter and came up with a bottle. Then she turned back to me.

"He can't go back, Chris. You know that, don't you?" she whispered.

"I'm sure somebody else can take you to the dance," I said, reaching for my fork.

"That's not what I meant," she said.

"Yeah, I know."

"What are you going to do?" she asked, sounding concerned and urgent.

I poured warm syrup over my blueberry pancakes. "Find him. That's what I came to do," I said.

"And after that?"

"Don't know." I honestly didn't.

"How will you find him?" she asked. "He hasn't even given me a phone number."

"I think I have a pretty good idea of where he is," I said. "I just have to get there."

"Well, I can't help you," she said. She seemed genuinely worried that I was going to take him away from her. "I really don't know where to find him."

I smiled. Win had certainly, to quote my mother, made an impression on this girl.

"I don't need you to tell me where he is," I said between mouthfuls. "But I could use your help finding a ride—I missed the stop last night or this morning. Fell asleep."

She stared at me, arms splayed on the counter. I could see her weighing it out. She ignored two requests for refills before she spoke. "Which way you going?"

"East. Near a town called Browning. About thirty miles past the park," I said. I watched her face for any sign of reaction.

"Browning?" she said. "That's close to sixty miles. And over the pass."

I nodded.

"He's been riding all that way?"

I shrugged. "You'd know better than I would."

She failed to hide the smile. To her credit, she didn't look away, either. "What are you going to do?" she repeated.

I shrugged. When I'd left Atlanta, I'd come out here to drag Win back. I'd come to punish him for this, his last act of selfishness and inconvenience. Now I wasn't sure.

"I guess I'll figure that out when I see him," I said.

"What about that guy?" she asked.

"I don't know. I only figured out he was following me last night."

Her eyes stayed fixed on mine as she spoke. "Earl?" she said softly.

"Yeah, Danni?" replied the man sitting to my immediate left.

"You've heard all this, right?"

"Yep."

I panicked. Would this guy tell someone?

"You heading back home this morning?" she asked, still staring at me.

"Only if I get another cup of coffee. Got up at four this morning to deliver that load to Kalispell, and if I don't get some more caffeine, I'm going to put the truck in a ditch halfway home," he said.

Danielle grabbed the coffeepot, filled his cup. "Think you could drop my friend here at Browning?"

Earl nodded. "Be doing me a favor. Little conversation is a hundred times better than the caffeine," he said.

"I'd appreciate that," I said, rising off my stool. "I'll go grab my bag from the bus."

"Don't hurry. Nothing waiting for me at home but a field to plow."

Danielle kept her eyes fixed on mine, like she was trying to decide if she was doing the right thing. I threw a ten-dollar bill on the counter next to my plate. The tip was more than I could afford, but I figured it was the safest way to try and let her know that maybe we were on the same side.

I stopped short. "Wait," I said, sitting back down. "That guy has his own car. He's just going to follow us—"

"I'll take care of him," she said calmly as the bell rang and she whirled around to grab another pair of plates.

She'd take care of him? What did that mean?

186

"How?"

"Just go on out and get your stuff off the bus," she ordered as she walked toward the other end of the counter, dropping off one plate halfway down before stopping in front of my shadow.

"What's she doing?" I said aloud.

"Don't know," Earl offered, "but it'll work."

Jacketman lowered his paper as Danielle slid the plate onto the counter. "More coffee?" she asked just a little too loudly.

The guy nodded.

She turned, grabbed a different pot, shot me a look that told me I'd better get ready to bolt, and spun around.

"Watch this," Earl muttered.

I did. She moved as gracefully as she had been all morning, those long legs carrying her confidently from kitchen to counter like a dancer navigating difficult choreography. If I hadn't been paying attention, I wouldn't have noticed how she short-stepped and caught her toe on a milk crate on the floor beneath the soda dispenser. I wouldn't have noticed that she already had the coffeepot tipped forward before she even reached the counter. Wouldn't have noticed how she caught herself but still managed to launch a half-full pot of decaf across the plate and into Jacketman's chest and lap.

Good thing I was paying attention.

"That'll do it," Earl said.

I looked away. But out of the corner of my eye I could see Jacketman jump backward off his stool.

"Ohmygosh," Danielle shouted. "I am *so* sorry."

The floor waitress rushed over with a napkin dispenser.

Danielle tugged the towel out of her waistband and tried to reach over to pat the man dry.

It was hopeless, though. The guy was soaked, stained light brown from chest to midthigh.

He grabbed the towel. "You . . . ," he began, but couldn't seem to finish.

"I'm so sorry," she repeated, and I almost believed her. "I'll totally pay for the cleaning, or your breakfast, or whatever."

The other waitress said something to the man and began ushering him toward the bathroom. He glared at Danielle, threw a glance my way, and let himself be pushed toward the men's room.

When he was out of sight, Danielle turned and crossed back to us. "Go get your stuff, then hide out back in my car—the red Jeep—until the bus leaves. Wait till Earl comes round to get you."

"I can't believe you just did that," I said as she grabbed a handful of clean rags and dunked them in a sink full of soapy water.

"It wasn't fresh. Halfway cold," she said, shrugging. "Go."

"Are you sure this will work?" I asked, shoving a last bite of pancake into my mouth.

"Girl said go, son," Earl said. "I'll see you in a while."

"Thanks," I said.

Danielle passed through the open space in the counter, heading toward the mess she'd made. She slowed as she passed me, looked into my eyes.

"I hope I didn't just punk the FBI so you could take Win back," she said.

"You didn't. I'll make sure he gets you a corsage," I said.

"Son, I think *you'd* better get her a corsage," Earl said.

"Go now," she whispered.

I raced outside, tried not to look like I was running across the lot, and circled to the back side of the bus. I pushed on the door. It didn't budge.

The driver had locked it up.

Crap.

CHAPTER TWENTY-TWO

"Eagle! Get up!" Win shouted.

"Five more minutes, Mom," I mumbled.

"Five more minutes and Morgan will have eaten all the processed pork products. You wouldn't want that, now, would you?" he said.

I looked over the edge of the loft. Win was already packed and dressed. He was never ready before me. After stuffing my bag back into the sack and rolling up my pad, I chucked them over the edge of the loft and then moved toward the ladder. I was sore everywhere. Bruises mottled my arms and legs like lace.

I pulled on a T-shirt. "How long you been up?"

"Long enough to look around. This place is amazing."

I studied my friend. His bruises matched my own, but he also sported a sizable knot just above his left eye. I slipped my feet into my shoes and strapped my sleeping bag onto the bike, then followed Win out of the barn to breakfast.

Effie dropped the skillet she was pouring gravy from when we walked into the kitchen.

"What happened?" she shrieked as she looked us over.

I shrugged. What the hell had happened, anyway?

"Nothing," Win said. "Really."

Effie stared at us, apparently unaccustomed to such a smooth liar as Win.

"But you two look like—"

"Effie, the boys said it was nothing. Let it be."

Her face flushed as she smoothed a stray silver hair back into place and gestured toward the table. Morgan had already begun to eat. We ate quickly, Win and I again packing more food into our bellies than anyone might have thought possible. Biscuits. Gravy. Sausage. Eggs. Ham. We ate in relative silence, the entire meal like one of those awkward pauses that had punctuated our easy evening the night before.

"You should make Glacier by noon," Morgan said without looking at either of us.

I nodded as I sopped up egg and gravy with the nub of a biscuit. "Good. Shouldn't put us too far behind."

And that was the extent of the conversation. Minutes later Win and I were on our feet, saying polite good-byes to our hosts, hauling the paper bag Effie thrust into my hands.

"Just a light lunch," she said as I accepted a parcel that weighed at least as much as my front pannier.

We thanked her, accepted her embraces, and followed Morgan out to the porch and our bikes.

He shook our hands. "Good luck to you boys," he said solemnly.

"Thank you," Win said. We stood awkwardly for half a minute. Something inside Effie's lunch bag was seeping through the paper bottom.

"If you're ever back this way," Morgan said, "be sure to come by."

I nodded. Win reached for his helmet. "See you later, Morgan."

Sixty miles and five hours later we arrived. We'd stopped only for a short and very cold swim in a lake at the eastern edge of the park. The glacial melt eased the soreness from last night's grudge match.

"What do you want to do now?" Win asked me as he unpacked the contents of Effie's lunch. The bag had made the journey tied precariously to his handlebars, dark purple goo dripping a trail as we rode.

"Eat," I said. "Stare at that," I added, pointing at the view. We were looking out at the canyon, the cars snaking up the ribbon of pavement known as the Going-to-the-Sun Road. We'd just climbed it, exulting in the fact that the ascent didn't wind us as much as we'd expected it to, as much as it would have nearly two months ago when we started this trip. Now I enjoyed the full heat of the early-afternoon sun drying the cold water out of my bike shorts.

"Yeah," Win said. "I think this is what they call basking."

I grabbed one of the blueberry turnovers that had been leaking, took a bite. "Basking."

I don't know if Glacier National Park was ever something I'd even thought of before we realized it was on our route to Seattle. I don't think I'd ever even heard of it, but now it felt like something we'd discovered. Sure, we'd been honked at by a hundred cars that thought we were crazy to take our bikes up the steep, exposed highway. And sharing that bit of road with giant, foul-smelling RVs hadn't been that fun. But the scenery, the pure exertion, the scale of it all, had resurrected a sort of epic quality that I'd forgotten the trip could hold.

And it was going a long way toward helping us forget last night.

"How long can we stay here?" Win asked me.

I shrugged. "When's your uncle expecting us?"

He hesitated. "Next week sometime. I think I told him the first of August, or so."

"Do you want to call him? Have you called him?"

Again hesitation, as if there was something he wanted to say but didn't. "Nah. He's pretty laid back. When do you have to go for orientation, college boy?"

"I'm not the one going Ivy League," I said.

Win ignored me.

"Orientation's on the fourteenth. I have to catch the bus back by the fifth at the latest," I said.

He nodded. "If it takes us a week to get over the Cascades and then head south into Seattle, I'd say we've got just today here."

For the first time on the trip I knew regret. Regret that we'd wasted so much time in less impressive places during the early part of our trip. If we'd known how amazing it would be out here, we probably would have ridden a little faster, taken a more direct route. And now the ride was almost over. But I was also feeling a bit relieved. Finishing was a sure thing now.

"Let's find a campsite, ditch the gear, look around," Win said.

I nodded. "But nothing illegal—they get pretty tweaked about that kind of thing in these places."

"As if the admission fee we paid wasn't bad enough," Win said. "How pathetic is that, by the way? Charging us the rate for a car? I mean, we're doing a good thing for the planet here. We're saving the environment from emissions on the most efficient machines in the world, and yet they still charge us the same usage fee as one of those rolling duplexes that all the blue-hairs are backing into each other—"

"Shut up," I said as something large pushed out of the brush fifteen feet from where we sat.

"Whoa," Win said as a snowy mountain goat emerged from the thicket.

"That thing's huge," I whispered. We both watched the goat in silence. Probably three feet high at the shoulder, long white coat, powerful legs, serious-looking horns.

"Awesome."

I nodded.

"No, really. That thing looks, like . . . *regal*."

He was right. The animal had a presence that would have inspired reverence even without those horns.

"But what's it doing down here?" I whispered.

The goat ignored us as it walked over to a spot where a foot-path broke from the parking lot into the brush. It sprang onto the asphalt. Immediately it looked less impressive, stacked up next to the station wagons and SUVs.

We turned and watched it navigate through the lines of cars, hooves clicking distinctly on the pavement like the clips on the bottoms of my bike shoes.

Even in its less impressive surroundings, it was still pretty cool. I tried to enjoy it as much as I could, knowing that as soon as the tourists saw it, we'd be covered up in amateur wildlife photographers.

The goat sniffed the ground. "What's it looking for?" I asked.

Win shrugged.

And then the goat came upon a space where a giant RV had been parked only a few minutes ago. This one had left behind a puddle of antifreeze—a two-foot-wide neon green stain on the pavement. I took small consolation in the fact that the motor home might be disabled somewhere.

As soon as the goat entered the stall, it made straight for the pool and began licking it up.

Perfect.

"We come all the way out here, and we get to see a goat lick up antifreeze," I muttered.

But Win was stage-whispering in a ridiculous British accent, "The *Mountainus goatus* is a unique species, known for its keen appetite for automotive fluids. Some attribute its longevity to the pickling properties of these agents. And isn't this one a beaut?"

By now a crowd was forming around the animal. Families with cameras. A kid started pelting it with Oreos, until a ranger came and broke up the show. Visitors dispersed reluctantly, snapping photos as the ranger shooed the goat away.

She saw us sitting by ourselves, bikes leaned against each other, and walked over.

"How long you guys been riding?" she asked.

"About seven weeks," Win said. "Took off from West Virginia."

She raised her eyebrows in appreciation. "You've made good time."

We absorbed her compliment silently.

"I see you've met Eddie, our resident drug-addicted goat," she said. "He's crazy. Harmless, but that's probably more of a problem than the crazy part."

"How's that?" I asked.

"My name's Rita, by the way," she said, sounding a little annoyed.

Rita was too old for us to hit on. We only asked names when girls were young. And cute. "Sorry. Chris," I said, pointing at myself before hooking a thumb at Win, "Winston."

She nodded. "Harmless is worse than crazy because he can't defend himself. Doesn't know people aren't good for him, just keeps a range of about a mile around this parking lot."

"He never goes up into the mountains?"

She shook her head. "Not as far as we can tell. Nothing he can lick up there that might corrode his brain. We've tried three times to relocate him, but he always comes back. He's sort of forgotten how to be a mountain goat."

"What, he's like a big, stupid house dog?" I asked.

Rita nodded. "With really dangerous horns."

Win finally spoke. "What's going to happen to him?"

Rita picked up a corner of an Oreo wrapper and put it in her pocket. "Park management is talking about putting him down. It'd be a shame, though. It's not his fault he's like this . . . ," she trailed off. "Well, I've gotta get back to work. If you see him again, try to shoo him away. He'll go if you take a good run at him," she said.

The thought that I might be able to scare him away made me even sadder.

"You guys camping here tonight?" she asked.

"Yeah."

"Try the lodge at Lake McDonald. They let cyclists crash in the bus driver barracks for free."

"Thanks," I said.

I watched her go. When I turned back, Win was still staring at the spot where Eddie had disappeared into the brush.

"Win?" I said.

"Yeah," he said quietly, still staring after the goat.

"You all right, man?" I asked.

He didn't respond. I recognized the feel of the coming moment. Didn't want to climb back in. It was shaping up like the night at the church, finding the money in his saddlebag, last night in the barn. It felt like, well, like *distance*. I didn't want to see where it led this time.

"Win? You been sampling the antifreeze with old Eddie?" I asked.

Dumb jokes. Always the escape hatch. Win turned and faced me. It was like I'd thrown a switch.

"Lake McDonald, right? Let's check it out. I feel like another swim anyway," he said, springing up and going to his bike. I watched him walk away, feeling more and more like I was watching a stranger.

CHAPTER TWENTY-THREE

After a moment of panic and a frantic search for anything resembling a normal keyhole with a pickable lock (not that I knew how anyway), I glanced back at the diner. I could see Danielle pouring coffee at a corner booth, keeping an eye on me.

Think.

I scanned the sides of the bus. The rest of my stuff was on board. It wasn't much, but I couldn't afford to leave it either. And if they discovered it when the bus stopped in Spokane, Jacketman would know I'd gotten off long ago instead of just managing to slip away in a crowded bus terminal.

I circled around to the other side of the bus and found what I was looking for: a slightly open window an aisle or two ahead of my own. I hopped up, grabbed the exposed lip, and eased my left hand over, sliding the window in its track to widen the opening. My hands were cramping by the time I had it open enough, and I dropped down to shake them out. Ignoring the stiffness that had crept into my back after trying to sleep in my seat, I hopped back up, planted my feet on the side of the bus, and cranked with my upper arms to lever myself in.

Sometimes it pays to be the skinny guy. It wasn't graceful, and I'm glad no one could see me from the diner. Someone passing on the highway honked, but that was it. Maybe twenty seconds later I spilled onto a seat filled with someone's knitting bag and crawled into the aisle.

I hustled back, grabbed my stuff from the seat, and hurried out my window, dropping to the asphalt as quietly as I could manage. I crept up to the front of the bus. Danielle was back behind the counter. Jacketman's stool was still empty.

The other passengers were paying their bills and drifting out to the bus. I saw the driver rise from his stool. Jacketman still hadn't left the bathroom. I walked as calmly as I could across the lot and around the back of the building, where I found Danielle's Jeep waiting as promised. I tugged open the back door, climbed in, and slouched down, breathing for what seemed like the first time since I left the diner.

Ten minutes later I watched from her car as the bus pulled out of the lot, followed thirty Mississippis later by Jacketman's sedan. When they were both out of view, Danielle came out the back door.

"Nice work," I said.

She shrugged. "Thanks. But if he's FBI, we're all in major trouble."

"You underestimate yourself," I said.

She rolled her eyes. "Whatever. Earl's out front. Give him gas money if you can. His crop sucked this year."

I nodded. "Okay," I said, reaching for my bag.

"What are you going to do when you find him?" she asked again.

I had no idea.

"Thanks for your help," I said, dismissing her question.

She crossed her arms. "Don't make me regret it."

Jeez, she was hot. "I'll try not to."

"I can drop you at Browning, all right," Earl was saying between fiddling with the radio and shuffling the toothpick back and forth across his lips.

"Actually, the farm's somewhere along this highway. Guy named Morgan lives there. I'm not sure how close to Browning it really is," I said.

He nodded. "I know Morgan's place. My farm's another twelve miles past his, so I can take you up to the front door if you like."

"That'd be great," I said, staring out the window. The landscape looked different. Maybe it was because I was traveling east, maybe it was the change in the color of the leaves and the way the wheat had grown gold in the autumn sun. Earl found Patsy Cline on the radio, "Crazy." Maybe I was.

Earl didn't try to talk. As we rode, I kept waiting for him to initiate some conversation, feeling tense and apprehensive about what I'd tell him. But apparently he'd heard enough while eaves-dropping on Danielle and me in the diner. As the miles slipped by, I began to relax and appreciate the silence.

As a George Jones song died away, Earl pulled to the side of the road. I could see the farmhouse, the barn a half a mile away. We'd covered the fifty miles in just under an hour.

"There's Morgan's spread," Earl said, the engine idling hard.

"That's it," I agreed.

We both surveyed it for a moment. "Want me to take you up the driveway?" he asked.

I shook my head. "No . . . but thanks."

I opened the door of the truck. I pulled my last ten out of my pocket and placed it on the dash. Earl didn't object. "What're you gonna say to him?" he asked.

The door fell shut, and I reached into the bed of the truck to grab my pack. "Thanks for the ride, Earl," I said, no more sure of how to answer his question than I was about what I'd do when I found Win.

The place was like I remembered. Save for the fact that those pea fields that had lined the road were now empty, the soil freshly tilled, tanging the air with the scent of earth. I followed the gravel driveway up to the farmhouse, which looked as if it had been painted since I left. Somehow the half-mile walk felt longer than it should have. With every step, with every shift of gravel beneath my feet, the question my father, Vanti, Danielle, Earl—everybody—had been asking echoed.

What are you going to do, Chris?

I still had no answer when I reached the end of the drive, where I found Morgan sitting on the front porch, hair slicked down, wearing a clean pair of jeans and a pressed shirt. When I was a few yards from the steps leading up to the screen door and where he sat on a bench, he finally spoke.

"Thought that might be you," he said. I was sure he'd been watching my approach since the truck stalled on the shoulder of the highway. Sure that he'd been awaiting my return along with Win.

"Good to see you, sir," I said. And I meant it. Morgan had a calming way about him. Somehow the fact that he didn't make a big deal about my arrival made it easier.

"You too, Chris." Honestly, the man acted as if I'd seen him yesterday, instead of almost two months ago.

"Where's Effie?"

"In the house—on the phone. We're on our way into town. Gotta go see a man at the bank about something. She told me to sit here and not get dirty until we left."

I laughed. "You get that tractor running yet?" It seemed like the only thing to ask. What if Win wasn't here? What if my hunch had been wrong?

He nodded—only once. "Yep. Not long after you boys came through. Crop turned out well. Don't know if I'd have gotten it in alone, though." He looked at me, then away, picked at an imaginary speck of something on the starched denim of his trousers. Everybody was protecting Win.

"He's in the barn, Chris," he said. "I think you remember where it is."

I nodded. "Thanks." He was as torn about my finding Win as I was. And maybe he knew that since I'd come that far on my own to find him, finishing the rest of the journey alone made sense. He'd known that this summer about the bikes, and this wasn't much different.

I started walking toward the barn, left him sitting there on the porch. I heard him call over my shoulder. "I didn't ask him to stay," he said. After a beat he added, "But we've been glad to have him around."

I hesitated.

"What are you going to do, son?" he asked.

I didn't turn as I called out to him. "Catch up with an old friend, sir," I said, striding toward the barn.

CHAPTER TWENTY-FOUR

"Truck on a triangle, baby!" I shouted, pointing to the diamond shaped road sign at the crest of the pass.

"Fourteen percenter!" Win said as we began picking up speed.

"We earned it after that climb," I said.

We careered downhill on the empty road in silence for a full minute, enjoying the speed and roar of the wind in our ears.

Then Win returned to a favorite subject. "That Danielle was hot."

"You sort of said that already," I pointed out. "In fact, you've said it about thirty times a day for the past week."

It was true. Since we'd left that truck stop and made our way through a flat patch of eastern Washington before heading up the mountain road, Win had been talking about Danielle. At

Ross Lake, Win talked about Danielle. At the salmon hatchery, more Danielle.

"I'm getting a little bored with this conversation," I said.

Win laughed. "Only 'cause she liked me better."

"I'm the one who got us the fries," I said.

"But I'm the one who got her address," he said. That part was true. But what was he going to do? Write her letters and keep talking about her all the way into freshman year?

"So, what's the plan when we hit Seattle?" I asked. "We're only going to have a day there before we have to catch the bus back."

Again Win acted as if he was going to say something but caught himself. "Not sure. I guess there's that Space Needle thing," he said. "Sort of a landmark, right?"

"Yeah. But I'm kind of tired of the touristy crap. Winthrop did me in."

"What are you talking about? That fake shoot-out was cool," Win said.

The whole town had been fake. Old storefronts built over new . . . wooden sidewalks . . . blacksmiths . . . saloons. We'd rolled in just before lunch, as crowds gathered near an ice-cream shop/espresso bar. Seconds later two fake cowboys rushed out and started shooting at each other.

"Whatever. Bet the Space Needle costs money," I pointed out. My reserves had dwindled, and I needed to save enough to get my bus ticket home and eat on the three-day drive. And I was still waiting for Win to pay me back. For that matter, I was still waiting for him to explain the wad of cash in his saddlebag.

"My treat," he said. "There's also that market."

"The one where they throw the fish around?" I asked.

He nodded. "That's the one."

We rode quietly for a space, enjoying the long, effortless slide down the mountain. This section of our ride had been full of rocky crags, snowcaps, evergreens, and pale blue skies. The air was so clean it almost burned to breathe it. According to the map, the next decent-size town we'd drop into was poetically called Concrete. Though the name was ugly, I couldn't imagine the place would be.

I didn't have time to share this thought with Win before I saw the furry brown shape on the left shoulder of the road, nuzzling the pavement.

Win saw it too. "Bear?" he whispered, applying his brakes.

"Can't be," I said, doing the same.

It wasn't. From where we stood now, fifty yards uphill, it was plainly a coyote. We could clearly see now that it was about the size of a collie. It was picking through the remains of an opossum. Though we'd been hearing coyotes for weeks when we stopped to camp, this was the first time I'd seen one.

"This is way cooler than the auto goat," Win said. "A real, live wild animal."

"Totally. Although I'm not sure how wild a state highway can be considered," I said. Win smiled. We watched it tear apart what appeared to be small intestine.

"Kind of weird it's out in the daytime, isn't it?" Win asked.

I shrugged. "Maybe. They're supposed to be pretty skittish of people."

"Think it's going to do anything else besides play with its food?"

I shrugged.

"Shall we, then?" he asked.

"Just a sec," I said, unzipping my camera from the handlebar bag. Win fished his out as well, and we both snapped quick photos.

"I'm going to see if I can get a closer shot as we ride past," I said as I put my foot back into my pedal and started rolling down the mountain behind Win, who'd already stowed his camera away. Already the slope was evening out. The river in the valley was no longer a shining, wet ribbon. Now it had detail and seemed to have grown wider since I first glimpsed it from below Diablo Dam. We'd be pedaling instead of coasting soon.

As we pulled past where the coyote was eating, it looked up.

"Hey," Win said. "It's saying good-bye."

But it wasn't saying good-bye. With surprising speed it shot across the road toward us, ears laid back and teeth bared.

"Go!" I shouted. The coyote was ten feet away and closing fast as I fumbled for my gears, dropping the disposable camera in my hurry. It bounced behind me and into the rut between the shoulder and the hillside.

Win looked over his shoulder. "Do coyotes get rabies?"

"Don't really want to find out!" I shouted, rapidly clicking through my shifter to find my highest gear.

The animal was close enough that I could hear it snarling.

"Good dog!" Win shouted to it, testing our usual first line of defense with dogs that chased us.

"It's not a Labrador!" I said.

"Same genus! Got a better idea?" he asked, tugging his water bottle from its cage and uncapping it with his teeth. I did the same. If the fact that it was a canine meant it bore any similarity to the other dogs that had chased us, this would probably do the trick. We both turned the bottles toward the coyote and started squirting.

Most of our shots fell short. A few hit it on the flanks. Either way, it was slowing down. Win launched a stream that hit it smack in the left eye, and it pulled up sharply.

"Hah! Take that, you rabid little intestine-eating bastard!" I screamed as the coyote dropped about twenty feet behind us.

My bottles were both empty. "I'm out," I said, looking back to see the coyote falling farther behind. He stopped altogether for a few seconds, mounted a halfhearted attempt to run us down, but gave up as gravity pulled us safely away.

"I think we've lost him," Win said.

"Yeah, but keep pace for a while, just to be sure. . . ."

Adrenaline still coursed through me.

"How fast are we going?" I asked Win after another half a mile had slipped past.

Win glanced at the cycling computer mounted to his handlebar. "Forty-nine," he said.

"That's faster than we've ever . . . ," I started to say, but then felt the telltale sensation of my rear tire dancing sideways. I was losing speed.

"Flat!" I yelled over the rushing wind.

"Flat!" I shouted again when he didn't respond, the space between us stretching as I glanced behind us. No coyote chasing at our heels. "The coyote's gone, Win," I said as I applied my brakes, afraid that if I let the tire sink any lower at this speed, I'd damage the rim.

He turned and looked at me, ducking his head between his arm and the handlebar. But he didn't stop.

He didn't even slow down.

"Win!" I shouted again, anger edging out any of the fear that had been there before.

He sat up on his seat, shouted over his shoulder in a voice that carried back to me like an echo. Like he was already gone. "You'll catch up," he said, adding, "Someday."

I was stunned. Catch up? Someday?

"Win!" I shouted again. "You bastard!" But he was already disappearing behind a bend in the highway. For the first time in nearly two months I was completely alone.

And I had no idea why. Win was a flake, but for most of my life I'd known I could count on him completely. For the last eight weeks I'd known that more than ever. And now he'd left me, with a flat tire, no water, and a rabid coyote looking for an easy snack.

I hopped off my bike and started the routine I'd practiced dozens of times across country. I actually waited half a second once I had all the tools out. But Win wasn't there to time me. I dug into my patch kit.

"What the . . . ?"

No patches. I'd just bought a new set last week. I hadn't used that many. One flat yesterday. Maybe another I'd forgotten. But not five.

Win.

"Bastard!" I swore again as I dug deeper into my bag, unpacking the whole left pannier to find one of the spare tubes we kept in the bottom. Replacing a tube took longer than simply edging out a section of it to patch. I'd replaced only three tubes the entire trip across, and those were on ones that couldn't be repaired because the stem had gotten tweaked or torn. Tubes, compared with patches, were expensive. And when you used up your tubes, you could be stranded. It was my last one.

But I had no choice. I worked the tire off the rim with my tire irons, ripped the old tube out, and found the sliver of amber glass from a broken beer bottle still stuck in the housing of my tire.

I don't know how long it took me to replace the tube and get back on the road. I do know that my heart had stopped pounding, and now all I was feeling was rage toward the guy I'd been trusting with my life the whole way across the country. I climbed back onto the seat of my bike and started pedaling, quickly picking up speed as the incline pulled me forward.

What would I say to Win when I found him? Maybe I'd just hit him. Hit him and flatten both his tires and then leave *him* behind. Revenge fantasies carried me all the way down the hill, past a half-burned, crumbling trailer next to the side of the road, and were still percolating as I pulled into a gas station next to a sign welcoming me to Concrete, population 790.

I didn't see Win, but I needed water, so I got off my bike, grabbed my bottles, and unclasped my chinstrap.

A tiny little woman was perched on a plastic folding chair, her head dwarfed by a broad straw hat and a pair of dark glasses.

"Got any water?" I asked.

She swept a gnarled arm around in a backward arc. "Round back's a tap. Help yourself," she said between sips of her coffee.

I walked in the direction she'd pointed and found the tap as promised. The rusted wheel stuck for a second before the water began to trickle out in a slow stream. I uncapped a bottle, held it under, and leaned against the wall, my head inches from a window ledge peeling paint in giant flakes. I closed my eyes; the aftermath of the adrenaline rush had left me drained.

The cool water spilling over the top of my bottle and onto my hand made me open my eyes abruptly. When I did, I saw something that made me ignore the puddle of water forming around my feet.

On the sill of the window just in front of me were five adhesive patches lined up in a neat row.

My patches.

Win.

I turned off the spout, capped my bottle, and grabbed the patches. I charged around to the front of the building. The woman was still sitting in her chair.

"How long ago was he here?" I demanded.

She seemed confused, then she stirred herself enough to speak. "Kid on the bike? Maybe ten minutes ago."

I caged my water bottle, stashed the patches into my saddlebag, locked my left pedal in place, gave a push, swung the right leg over, and rode west.

CHAPTER TWENTY-FIVE

I rounded the corner of the house and headed for the open barn doors. I could hear the sound of hammering inside. The back fields still bore the scars of the harvest—deep ruts left behind by the tractor wheels.

The hammering was steady, insistent, my heartbeat falling into rhythm with the pounding. Even in this open space it felt like my world had collapsed again to this barn.

Win was standing in the barn, his back to me, bent over a pair of sawhorses laden with two-by-fours. He looked taller. I was mildly surprised to find him not in a pair of bike shorts and a jersey, but wearing a pair of grubby Carhartts and a ratty T-shirt I didn't recognize. I realized then that I'd sort of frozen him in my mind as I'd seen him on the day he disappeared—bike shorts, gray shirt, cycling shoes, helmet—looking like he had every day of our trip. But of course, he'd changed.

"Hey, Win," I said.

He stopped hammering at the sound of my voice. He was standing exactly where we had wrestled a month and a half ago. Had it only been that long?

He didn't turn at first, just rested his palms on the board he was nailing and said, "I knew you'd come."

I dropped my pack and sat down on a crate near the open door. "What tipped you off? Could it be that you pretty much told me where you were?" The anger crept into my voice unbidden. It had always been there, and now that its source was standing in front of me, it was drawn out like a magnet.

Win didn't seem to notice. "Might have been that," he said. He turned, and I could see he'd let the stubble he'd started this summer grow into a full-blown beard. The cut on his face from the night we fought had knit itself into a neat scar. His hair was longer.

Win looked happy. More than happy—peaceful.

It took me completely by surprise.

"What?" he said. I hadn't realized I was staring.

I shook my head. "Nothing. You look different . . . that's all."

He nodded. "Probably. So do you. You look older."

"I guess I am. My birthday was last month."

"Yeah, I remembered," he said, moving to a low stool across from my perch. "Thought about calling."

"Really," I said without interest. Now that I was here, I didn't want to pull the trigger.

We were both quiet for a moment. "Remember that time you

had that birthday party at the mini-golf place, and the manager yelled at us for doing that thing with the club and the clown?"

I actually smiled. "Yeah, but it was totally you. I just got blamed for it."

He laughed. "Sort of like this, huh?"

I nodded. "Yeah. Sort of."

Then we were quiet again. Win messed with the hammer, tossing it so it landed claw down in the dirt, over and over again. Finally I spoke. "What are you doing here?"

He sighed. "Harvesting, mainly. Now that that's done, I'm just sort of doing a few odd jobs, building a new gate, clearing brush, working on the tractor when it breaks down—"

"Damn it, Win. That's not what I meant."

He let the hammer fall to the ground once more and looked me in the eye. "I know what you meant, Chris."

"Well, then why'd you let me come all the way out here if you're not going to answer my questions?" I said, my voice edging higher, louder than it needed to be.

"It's not like that, Chris," he began. "It's . . . complicated."

"Not really. I mean, your dad's a controlling prick. We've known that for years. You wanted to get away. College almost nine hundred miles from home wasn't quite far enough, so you hide out here."

He didn't say anything. Suddenly I had the sensation we were wrestling again.

"The part I'm still having trouble understanding is that you used me, Win. *You used me.* You knew all along you were going to stay out here, didn't you?"

"Not here exactly . . . ," he began.

"But you knew you weren't coming back. Definitely knew you had no uncle in Seattle."

"Yeah. Sorry about that."

"Sorry? You're sorry? That's classic! Screw everybody over and expect an apology to cover it?" I was shouting now.

He shook his head. "I didn't see any other way."

"You had twenty thousand dollars in your saddlebag, and this was the only way?"

"Heard about that, huh?"

"No. I found it the second week. In Indiana."

He looked surprised. I enjoyed the advantage. "Why didn't you say something?"

I still hadn't figured out how to answer that question. "How was this the only way to escape?"

"Not escape, exactly," he said. "The only way to get away and say good-bye at the same time."

Jacob and the angel all over again.

"Good-bye? Your parents think you're *dead*. At one point they suggested I murdered and robbed you! Now they're just convinced I know where you are or that I helped you plan all this. Your father's been to see me on campus. He's had his own personal FBI agent harassing me for the last month, Win!"

"You know how he is, Chris . . . he'll lose interest in me after a while—"

I went for the pin. "He bought my dad's company."

Win fell silent, his mouth hanging open.

"He's going to fire him unless I give you up."

Win dropped his eyes and stared at the floor as we sat. He

stood up abruptly, walked over to the workbench, pulled a coffee can off the top shelf, and removed the lid. He withdrew an envelope. "This is for you," he said, crossing to me and dropping it at my feet. "I told you I'd pay you back."

"What is it?" I asked without reaching for it.

"The money I owe you. And a little more. I figured school's kind of expensive, and I didn't want you to have to pay for the bus tickets—"

"What the hell, Win? I don't want your money."

"Don't be an idiot, Chris," he said. "You need it."

"That doesn't mean I want it. You're just as bad as he is! What am I supposed to do? Take your money and feel grateful? Your dad's been trying to throw his money around, buy me off, and threaten my dad . . . but you? I never thought you were *that* much like him."

"I'm not like him!" he said.

"Of course you are! You're using people like he does. You're just acting like it's noble or that you had to do it. At least your dad has the balls to do it outright."

"Shut up, Chris," he started.

"It makes perfect sense that you came back to the place you figured they'd be happiest to see you, ask the fewest questions. They probably don't even mind being used. And I'll bet you haven't shared any of that money with them," I said.

"I mean it, Chris," he said.

"Or what?" I said. "Let's see what the old man has taught you. What kind of threats you can make?" My eyes stung, but still I stared at him, silently daring him to say the wrong thing, to give me a reason to do what I'd come out here for. "What have you got for me?"

"Do you want to know? Do you *really* want to know what he's taught me? Well, here it is. I'm pretty sure I could make him proud in the intimidation and manipulation department." His voice caught. "And that's what scares the crap out of me!"

That wasn't what I'd expected.

"I mean, even though I hate him, it scares the hell out of me how much I'm like him," he said.

"Way to face those fears head-on," I said. "Nothing like running away from home." I could feel my rage slipping away, like a slow leak in an overinflated tire. But part of me didn't want to let it go.

Win sprang to his feet, wiped his eyes, and began pacing the barn. "He's all talk, you know that."

I clenched my hands. "Right now his talk is pretty damn scary!"

"You know he won't do it, Chris."

"No, I don't. If he's all talk, why'd you stay out here? Why couldn't you handle it? Why do I have to take the heat? Why does my dad have to get fired?"

He shook his head. "The talk's enough when you hear it for as long as I have. I had to get someplace where his wasn't the only voice I heard inside my head. Someplace I could figure out who I was."

I didn't respond.

"When I said 'good-bye' before," he began, "I didn't mean to them. I meant good-bye to you. To us."

I nodded. Certain things between friends are said not because you don't know them, but because you need the other person just to say them.

"But here I am," I said, softening a bit more. "As good-byes go, this one's a bit unconventional."

"Here you are," he agreed. "I tried to tell you on the road, Chris. I did. Every time you asked about my uncle or we talked about school . . ."

"But you didn't," I said, throwing my hands up in the air. "If you had, I could have just told your dad you took off, and he might have left me alone."

"My dad would have come down on you even harder if I'd told you anything! And you can't lie, Chris. It would have been worse."

"But at least *I'd* have known! You should have told me!"

"I couldn't, Chris, and you know why. You'd have talked me into going back. You'd have been the one to make me see that I shouldn't do it."

"No," I said, shaking my head. "If you'd explained how bad it really was—"

"That's you *now* talking, Chris. We're both different people. I don't think I realized how different until after you'd gone. That trip changed us."

I nodded.

"*Now*, you know that I'm supposed to be here. *Then*, you would have done what you'd always done. You would have talked me off the ledge, told me I could get through it. And you'd have been right."

"But now?" I asked.

"Now," he said. "Now you and I both know that when you change as much as we have, when you've proved that you're more than everybody thought you were, you can't go back to the place you started. You've outgrown it all. The place, everybody's expectations . . . yourself."

He was right. And in the second that I realized it, I stopped fighting.

"Still, you could have told me," I said.

He picked the hammer up again, began pounding his palm. "I tried, Chris. I *really* tried. That day on the road with the coyote. That night in the barn. With the patches. When you passed me outside Concrete."

"You stayed in Concrete?"

He nodded. "Watched you ride past me. I hid in a stand of trees a quarter mile off the highway. Even with the flat and my head start I was pretty sure you'd catch me."

"Then, you never made it to the ocean," I said.

He shook his head. "Coast to coast, almost. But you made it. I knew you would."

The Win I'd spent the last decade with would never have admitted that. This incarnation was humble, even wise. We *had* changed. At least, he had.

"I knew you were up to something anyway," I said. "The money was sort of a clue. What kind of idiot carries around that much cash on his bike for two months?"

He laughed. "You were probably pretty pissed about me borrowing off you."

"Sorta," I said.

"I figured if I didn't keep being irresponsible Win, you'd really know something was up."

"That might have given it away," I admitted. I rubbed my hand through my hair—it felt sticky after those nights on the bus. A dog barked.

"What am I going to do, Win?" I said abruptly.

He shrugged. "Guess you know the answer to that question as much as I do."

"I came because I was pissed. I came here to take you back," I admitted.

"And now?"

"Not sure."

We sat in silence for a full minute.

"I don't even have to ask if you told anyone. I know that much about you, Eagle," he said, the old nickname feeling like a favorite pair of shoes. "I've thought a lot about why I sent you those postcards. I wanted to get a real good-bye in. That was part of it. I wanted to tell you I was sorry about leaving you. I wanted you to know I didn't use you."

"Thanks, I guess," I said.

"And I wanted you to see that I'm happy here, Chris. For the first time in my life I'm really happy. I work hard, earn my keep and a little more. Food's awesome . . ."

"Still sleep out here?" I asked.

He laughed. "No, they gave me his room."

I nodded.

"And they need me, Chris. I'm good for them."

"People need you there, too," I said.

He shook his head. "Dad needs me to carry on the family traditions of success and exploitation. Mom—well, Mom doesn't need much but a gold card. She'll be fine. Dartmouth probably has plenty of kids whose parents pulled strings to get them in."

He paused.

"That just leaves you, Chris. What about it? Do you need me? Anymore, I mean?"

CHAPTER TWENTY-SIX

The next morning I still hadn't caught Win. Somewhere in the afternoon of the previous day I'd been chasing him, I admitted that he'd ditched me.

I was so close to the coast that I could have made it the day Win and I got separated with little effort. But I took a number of side routes and back spurs off the main highway looking for my friend. At least, I told myself I was looking for him. But I knew then I'd never find him. Strangely enough, this realization didn't shock me as much as the real reason I made those detours.

I liked riding alone.

With the exception of the tent—which Win had still been carrying when we separated—I had pretty much everything I needed, including the stove and most of the food. The self-containment felt good, made me feel bigger, stronger.

I camped the first night on my own under a picnic shelter at a state park campground, my pad and bag on top of one of the tables. As I fell asleep, I decided to stop looking for Win. I decided not to go to Seattle.

And I decided not to call his parents. The last thing I wanted to do was get into it with Win's dad and listen to him tell me we should never have done this trip on our own. They probably would have insisted I stay put, wait for whomever they could hire or some local law enforcement to show up and help me look for Win. Or sent me to Seattle to meet him. And I wanted to see Win right now even less than I wanted to talk to his dad. I'd deal with all of that when I got back. Win might even beat me home.

Instead, I decided to enjoy my last few days of the ride. I would not stop. I'd come this far and still had time to make it to the Pacific.

I was content to ride the back roads and wander a little longer around the area. It was without a doubt the most beautiful stretch of road we'd yet seen on our journey. As barren as it had been east of the pass, it was that green and wet on this side. According to the locals, it never rained in the summer. All the same, the rivers I crossed were clean and wide, hemmed by lush evergreens, rhododendron, and laurel. And as I made it farther west—the foothills fading to soft mounds of green behind me, snowcapped mountains rising silently to the north and east—the scenery changed. The valley opened up into wide fields swaying with alfalfa and old Dutch barns standing sentinel over small herds of dairy cattle.

The morning after I camped at the state park, I reached the city limits of Sedro-Woolley. I veered off Highway 20 and followed a directional sign to the town center. Even though I was by myself—maybe because I was by myself—I wanted to stretch this out as long as I could. It was like a really good movie that I didn't want to end. I coasted slowly down the streets, past dozens of carvings of animals, pioneers, and totems, and hit a couple of small thrift stores before rejoining the highway.

When I reached the next town, Burlington, I was only twenty miles from the end of the highway in Anacortes. But I stopped here, too. I ate a giant burrito from an old Airstream trailer that had been converted into a restaurant. I found the bus station and learned that the next bus wasn't until midnight. I could catch local transit from Anacortes back to the main terminal and wouldn't have to backtrack. I bought both tickets and realized I had eleven hours to kill, more than enough time to finish my ride. The map showed a scenic drive that headed just north out of town.

It was about fifteen miles of two-lane blacktop hugging Chuckanut Mountain to the east and dropping right down into the ocean on the west. Vast teal water with no beach to speak of. I felt like a stunt driver on one of those car commercials. Glorious.

Then I caught a back road from Chuckanut to the highway spur leading to Anacortes. That road snaked through more farmland and tidal flats, past casinos and oil refineries. It turned out Anacortes was actually on an island—separated from the mainland by only a narrow channel. The map showed a city park as the westernmost point, so I followed signs to a small, rocky beach.

Land's end. On the long, boring stretches or grueling climbs I'd mentally rehearsed the moment I'd haul my bike across a sandy beach to dip my front wheel in the Pacific. But the shore was strewn with rocks and driftwood bleached white by sun and salt. I could see ferryboats crossing the water to distant islands. Things never turn out like expected. Sometimes they're better.

I caught myself thinking that Win would have liked this place. But I didn't miss him. Out on the road I'd realized something about us. As important as he was to me, and as strangely connected as we were, our friendship had almost gotten too tight.

I had this long-sleeved T-shirt in fourth grade that I wore all the time. There was nothing really special about it, but it was soft, had a picture of a guy surfing, and had been sent to me from Hawaii by my uncle. I loved it so much that I wore it for school pictures. I kept wearing it all year, through a five-inch growth spurt and my mom's protests that it was getting ragged at the edges. I was still hanging on to it when fall rolled back around. By then it was too snug and the sleeves hit just in the middle of my forearms. But it wasn't until I got that year's school pictures back and realized I'd worn the shirt again that I noticed how it was pinching at my neck and the outline of the surfer had faded into nothing.

I knew now that I had outgrown Win and my need for him, just like I'd outgrown that T-shirt. I'd hated giving up that shirt. I wasn't sure about giving up Win.

But it felt right to be there alone. The end of one journey and the beginning of another. One I had to make without that person who'd been the other half of me for the last ten years.

The sun was setting by the time I had removed my panniers from the front fork and extracted the front wheel. With it in hand, I picked my way over the boulders and logs to the shore. The water was clear, revealing pebbles, grit, and weeds swaying in the halfhearted tug of the waves. I crouched next to the edge, my toes inches from the waterline. I held the wheel in my right hand, extended out, the tire resting on the stones just beside me. Then I let it roll forward in my hand till the bottom edge made contact with the water, submerging the rim. It gleamed in the clear salt water.

"We made it," I said to no one. I stared at the water, at the sun dipping into the sea beyond the islands. "I made it."

The tide edged up and over my shoes and soaked into my socks. The water was colder than any Win and I had jumped into all the way across the country.

"It is water, after all," I said, this time to Win, wherever he was. Then I tossed my wheel onto the rocks behind me, sprinted forward into the water until it reached my hips, and let myself fall.

It was so cold that it burned. But I let myself stay under for a moment, the salt seeping into my eyes and nose. By the time I resurfaced and took my first real breath since the cold had splashed my ankles, I felt brand-new.

Now my journey had ended.

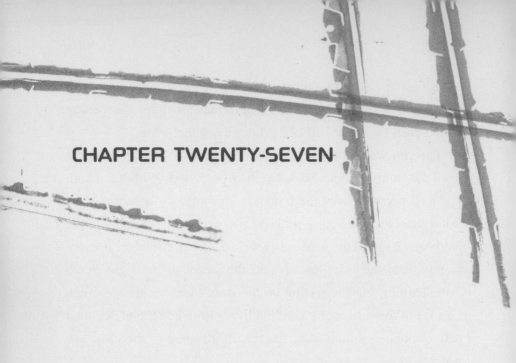

CHAPTER TWENTY-SEVEN

"Well?" Win said. "Answer the question. Do you need me anymore?"

I struggled. Wondered if I said yes, if he'd go back with me. "No, Win. I don't guess I do."

I didn't feel ashamed or sad to admit this fact. Win was ready to hear it because he'd stopped needing me. All the same, he was silent, almost reverent for a full minute.

"I'll be back someday," he said.

"If this Agent Ward or Jacketman has anything to say about it, it won't be long."

"Jacketman?" he asked.

"Another guy looking for you," I said.

"If they show up, I'll leave again. But I'll come home eventually. When I know I can be this version of me anywhere."

I nodded. "I don't think I'd be in a hurry to leave this place either."

He looked around the barn. "There's enough room to sort yourself out around here."

"That . . . and you've got a girlfriend," I said.

He smiled. "There is that."

"The Leaf Ball, though? Come on, Win. I thought we swore we'd never go to school dances. You're breaking a perfect record," I joked.

He looked at me. "*We* did say that."

I nodded, catching his emphasis. "She is hot," I admitted.

"Smart, too."

"She totally would have picked me, though," I said.

"All the more reason this town isn't big enough for the both of us," he said, laughing.

I nodded.

"What are you going to do, Chris?" he asked.

I shrugged. "Catch a bus home. Go back to my life, back to school."

"You happy there?" he asked.

I studied my hands. I thought about my classes. Vanti. "I can be," I said, adding, "Now."

"Take the money, Chris," he said, nodding toward the envelope lying at my feet. "Please."

I stared at it. I couldn't afford to be righteous here. And for some reason I didn't want to be anymore. "Yeah. Okay."

I leaned over and scooped it up. The envelope felt thicker than it should have. "Win, I don't think you owe me this much—"

"Forget it, okay?" he said.

"You've had this ready for me, haven't you?" I asked, waving the envelope at him.

He smiled. "Since I sent the first postcard. I actually thought you'd come sooner. Then I realized you'd have no way of knowing if I was in the same place."

"So you sent the others."

"Yeah. Figured you'd get here eventually."

I nodded. I was tired of talking about this. Tired of all of it.

"Got any food?" I asked.

Win smiled. "Best pies on Route Two."

Morgan and Effie were gone when we reached the house.

"Effie?" Win called.

"They went to the bank," I said. "I saw Morgan on my way to the barn."

He nodded and opened the fridge. "Apple or cherry?"

"Both," I said.

"Good man." He smiled as he backed away with a pie in each hand. He put a generous slice of each on two plates, poured two cups of coffee, and we sat. We talked as we ate, about nothing in particular, but I had the distinct feeling that I was not just catching up with an old friend, but also getting acquainted with a new one. I remembered how much I liked this guy. I saw again the things that had made him my best friend in the first place. Somehow those qualities were sort of all that were left.

We were still there at the table, the coffee long since cold, when

Morgan and Effie returned a couple of hours later. They came into the kitchen together. She gasped when she saw me sitting at her table again.

"Why, that's Chris!" Effie exclaimed, her hands flying to her cheeks. "Morgan, look! It's Chris, Win's friend!"

I stood and hugged her. "Hi, Effie."

She felt around my waist. "Still too thin, I see. I'll have to do something about that."

"The pie helped," I said, gesturing toward our dirty plates. Morgan took a seat at the table next to Win.

"But what are you doing all the way out here? Win said you were in school!"

Morgan shot me a look that warned me to choose my words carefully. Effie clearly had no idea what all this was about. Good for her.

"I was just in the neighborhood. Long weekend . . . thought I'd visit. But I'm running short of time."

"Well, you have to stay the night at least," she said. "You can't come all this way and not let me feed you," she insisted.

"Actually, I've got to catch a bus back today. I should get up to town and figure out when it leaves," I said.

She smiled. "But there's no bus east until late this evening," she said. "I know because I used to take it to visit my mother in Helena when Morgan couldn't drive me. Right?" She looked to her husband.

He nodded. "No bus until nine. I'd be happy to drive you into town tonight to catch it."

"But he can take the one tomorrow," Effie began.

"Chris said he needs to leave today, Effie," Morgan said quietly. "Don't bother him about it."

She looked hurt. "But—"

"The man knows his mind, Effie," Morgan said quietly. "Let it be."

I wanted to stay. It was easy to see what had drawn Win back here. But as tempted as I was, I knew it wouldn't be good for anybody.

"Well then, you'll just have to come back and visit some other time, won't you?" Effie said, looking near tears.

"Absolutely," I said. "I still dream about your cobbler."

This appeased her. "Then, I'd better get another one in the oven if it's going to have time to set up right before supper," she said, releasing me and reaching for a tea towel and tucking it into her waistband.

I smiled. "Please don't go to any trouble," I said.

"She lives for this kind of trouble, Chris," Morgan said.

Win nodded. They looked like they belonged together there at that table. Win looked far more at ease with Morgan than he ever had with his own father.

"Gate finished?" Morgan asked.

Win shook his head. "Almost."

"You want the truck? I could go finish that up if you and Chris want to get out of here for a while," he said.

Win looked at me and shrugged.

"Actually," I said, "I'd rather work on that gate. You can't trust important stuff like that to Win."

Morgan's shoulders convulsed in a bark of laughter. Win smiled.

"Well, when the gate's done, we've got a dead tree on the side of the little barn up in the woods. Needs to come down before it falls and does any damage."

"Sure," Win said. "You want us to split it for firewood, too?"

Morgan shook his head. "Not yet. Getting it down will take you up to supper. We'll split it later," he said, rising from the table. "I'm going to turn up the south fields with the disc plow."

Win and I left Morgan and Effie in the kitchen to return to the barn. His repair job was solid, and working together, it took us half an hour to finish the job and load it on the truck. We drove down a dirt road to the edge of the property to put it back on its hinges. After that we spent the rest of the afternoon climbing into the branches of a giant dead oak. We secured ropes to the heavier limbs, judged the angles, and tried to figure out how to keep the tree from falling onto the small barn it was so dangerously leaning over.

I was grateful for the work. Grateful for something to do with Win so we didn't run out of things to say to each other or dwell on old stories. The four or five hours we spent working together were full of purpose and honesty in a way that even our bike trip hadn't been.

Morgan came to watch us fasten the last of the chains to the tractor. Win climbed into the seat, turned the engine over, and edged it forward.

"Keep pulling," I shouted above the roar of the motor.

Morgan watched in silence as the tree came down exactly where Win and I had planned. It crashed to the ground, tossing dry leaves and twigs into the air, each root popping loudly as it pulled free from the earth.

Win killed the motor and joined Morgan and me where we'd assembled at the tree's side. It seemed even bigger now that it had fallen.

"That was a good one. Stood strong for years," Morgan said, kneeling next to the tangle of branches. He fingered a loop of frayed webbing, the remnant of a tire swing long gone. "But the time had come."

Win and I just nodded.

"Are you sure you can't stay the night?" Effie asked me again as we finished off the last of her cobbler.

"I'm sure," I said. It was a quarter past eight. Time to go.

Morgan nodded. "Then, we'd better get you up to Browning."

"I'll drive you," Win said, standing.

"Keys on the dash," Morgan said.

I hugged Effie half a dozen times, each time convincing her that I really had to go. Morgan walked us out to the truck, shook my hand. "It really was good to see you, Chris," he said to me as Win started the Chevy.

"Thanks," I said, adding, "For everything."

"We've always got plenty of work for you to do around here."

I smiled. "See you spring break, then."

Win and I said little for the first half of the short ride to town. Finally, when the lights of the tiny town center were in view, he began to speak.

"What are you going to do . . . at home? About me?"

I shrugged. "I'll figure something out."

"I don't like asking you to lie for me," Win said.

"I won't."

We pulled up in front of the bus stand.

"Guess this is me," I said.

Win nodded. He left the engine running as we climbed out of the truck. I tossed my bag over my shoulder.

"Got everything?"

I nodded. "Everything I came for, anyway."

Win smiled and held out his hand.

"You're a good man, Christopher Collins," he said.

"Likewise," I said, returning his handshake.

"What else do you say at a moment like this one?" he asked, still holding my hand.

I shrugged. "Not really a Hallmark card for these occasions."

"Guess not." He dropped my hand, tucked his fists under his arms I kept my gaze on my friend's eyes. He looked sad, proud, and satisfied all at once. It was like looking into a mirror.

Then he pulled his hands from his armpits and reached out and hugged me. The embrace surprised me.

"I'm glad you came," he said quietly.

"Me too."

We stayed like that for half a second more, before Win said, "We'd better let go now. If two guys hug this long in rural Montana, people start to talk about it."

I laughed, let him go for the last time, and turned toward the ticket counter.

CHAPTER TWENTY-EIGHT

Win gave me more money than he owed me or than I owed for the bus ticket on the credit card. I knew he'd done it on purpose—as a gift or maybe payback for what he'd put me through. If I'd looked in the envelope before he'd gone, I might have tried to give it back.

So when I got to the ticket counter, I asked for a week's pass. It cost a lot more than I could have afforded, but Win's money made the difference. School started again on Tuesday, so taking my time meant skipping at least one day of class, but no one was expecting me, and there was a whole lot of countryside I hadn't seen yet. I'd ridden the northern route enough—twice on a bus and once on a bike. I'd probably hurt somebody if I had to tread that ground again. It was time to find a new road.

The first bus I took went south. I got off and hitched my way into Yellowstone, knocked around for an afternoon, and then caught a ride to town with a young couple who'd been vacationing there. The next bus I caught took me all the way to St. Louis. I spent a morning there, went up in the arch in one of those tiny elevators, and then left. My last ride dropped south through a corner of Kentucky, over to Nashville, and finally ended up back in Atlanta, three miles from campus.

The scenery wasn't the only thing that changed. I was different too. I talked to other passengers. I made friends with a little kid whose mom was scarier than Win's dad. He kept popping over the seat in front of me, his chin on the headrest, and saying in this total hick accent, "You're my bud, ain'tchu?" I assured him that I was, even as his mom dragged him from the bus in the middle of Nebraska. I was remembering the person I'd been on the road and the fact that, unlike Win, I could be that guy anywhere.

Even at school. I guess that's why it felt right to skip my Tuesday classes. I just hoped nobody called home to report your absence, like in high school. I got back to Atlanta really early Wednesday morning, and took my time walking back to the dorm, grateful to be done with bus travel for a while.

When I got back to Armstrong, Abe Ward was sitting on the front stoop.

"What, are you on stakeout now?" I asked.

"Nice trip, Christopher?"

I'd sort of decided to forget about this complication during my return ride. I still hadn't figured out what I was going to tell everyone.

"Yeah," I said.

"Doesn't look like much stuff for a guy who's been back-packing for the last week," he said, pointing at the small day-pack slung over my shoulder.

"I travel light."

He nodded. "Anybody who can live off a bike for two months probably can. But still, I doubt you've got a sleeping bag in there."

Damn those investigative skills.

"What is that, maybe the second time you actually lied to me, Chris?" he asked. "You can give it up, though. I checked your credit card statement."

Crap.

"You bought a bus ticket for Omak."

"Yeah."

"But when my contact went to follow you from the station, you weren't on the bus."

"Is he the same one who you had following me around campus last week?"

He looked confused. "What?"

"The guy with the ugly jacket? Dice on the shoulder?"

He shook his head. "My contact's in the field office in Spokane. Looks like Win's dad tried to double-team you."

Win's dad had hired *another* investigator. Great.

"So you're either very smart or very lucky, Chris," Ward said, kicking at the corpse of a moth that had fallen to the brick floor.

"Neither," I said. That was true. I was glad I'd paid cash for the return ticket, though. If he'd checked that statement, he'd have been able to find Win within a few days.

"I guess I'd go with lucky if I were you," he said, leaning back against one of the round pillars supporting the porch roof.

I dropped my pack and sat down next to him. Neither of us spoke for a long time. As much as I didn't intend to give up Win, I knew I couldn't lie to Ward. Didn't have it in me. And I didn't want to. I'd just say nothing, given the choice.

"I'm good at this job, Chris. I can't speak for that other guy, but I'd have found you both out there if you'd gotten off in Washington. At least you've narrowed it down for me. I'm pretty sure that he's somewhere along the route you two traveled this summer, probably within two hundred miles or so in either direction. Since you lost him before you got to the coast, I'm also going to assume that he's farther back east than I might have thought earlier. And if I really give you the benefit of the doubt as a guy who popped a thirty-three on his ACT, I'd say you even bought that Omak ticket as a contingency. If I had to guess, I'd place Win somewhere in northwestern Montana or the Idaho panhandle."

I said nothing.

"So you can make it all go away right now or deal with another round of this mess." He paused a second, allowed me to weigh the option. "What's it going to be, Chris?"

I was silent. I still had no idea how to answer that question.

"Okay. Yes or no. Did you find him?"

Here was a question I could actually answer. A question I didn't have to lie in response to. Did I find him? Did I find the guy I'd been best friends with for the better part of my life? Did I find the guy I'd started that cross-country trek with this summer? Did I find the guy who'd been making my life so complicated for the last month? The guy I'd wanted to kill because his dad decided I already had? Did I find the guy Ward was looking for?

"Not exactly," I said.

Ward seemed genuinely taken by surprise. Possibly because he knew this was the truth. "What *exactly* did you find, then?"

I sighed. I've never really been one for the dramatic. Always preferred a simple answer to a direct question. Maybe it was the Boy Scout in me. But sometimes the truth is dramatic.

"Myself," I said.

"Excuse me?"

"You heard me," I said.

Ward shook his head. "Glad to hear that's working out for you," he said. But he didn't sound mad. He sounded *relieved*.

"You really didn't find Win?" he asked again.

"No," I said. "Not *really*."

Again he shook his head. "Funny thing, kid. But I've got a feeling Win just can't be found."

I looked up at him. He was smiling. "What about always getting the job done? Your perfect record? People always wanting to be found?"

He shrugged. "Maybe I was wrong. Maybe one black mark on a perfect record won't kill me."

I nodded.

"Hell, maybe I'm just bored," he said.

I smiled. Ward didn't want to find Win. He'd seen enough of Win's dad to know that Win's getting away might actually be a good thing.

"What are you going to do?" I asked him, aware that for the first time it was me posing that question about Win.

"Get back to my real job. Tell Coggans I pursued every possible lead but that Win is either dead or hidden so deep he can't be found unless he makes contact . . . something."

"Close enough," I said, adding, "On both counts."

He nodded. "Suppose so. I don't like to lie either."

I smiled.

"You'd have liked him," I said.

He laughed. "I expect I might have."

We sat quietly for half a minute.

"You smell like crap, Collins," he said.

I laughed. "Yeah. Six days on the Greyhound, no shower—"

"Please don't tell me any more," he deadpanned.

I stood. "Look, I've got a class this morning, and I really should get cleaned up. . . ."

"Yeah, I can't hang around here much longer asking you questions I don't want answers to."

"It was good to meet you, Mr. Ward," I said, extending my hand.

He took it, gripped it firmly. "You know Coggans won't give up easily," he said, adding, "he's bound to send more investigators."

"But they won't be as good as you, right? You're the best. Said so yourself."

"That I am," he said with a smirk.

"They'll give up easy."

"Probably."

He turned to go, descended the long concrete steps toward the parking lot. I watched him walk away. Halfway down he turned.

"Your name suits you," he shouted.

"What?"

"Your name. Christopher."

I shrugged.

"Christopher is the patron saint of travelers. Got that name for carrying a child across a stream—something about saving the kid's life. Ever since, he's been known to help those who wander. Folks pray to him all the time."

I took that in. It felt right, the fit surprising me.

"See you around, Saint Christopher," he said.

"Thanks," I called out as he disappeared from view.

I turned and strode through my dorm's doors, half a foot taller and a hundred pounds lighter. I took the steps up toward my hall two at a time, my legs buzzing slightly. Let them. Good or bad, I was ready for whatever came next.

In my room I pulled off my T-shirt and dumped out my pack, looking for the razor I'd packed but hadn't used during the trip. The dirty clothes, my lit book, and Win's envelope spilled onto the surface of the unmade bed. As I rummaged in the pile for the razor, I found something I knew I hadn't packed. Loose in the pile, between my first-aid kit and a small notebook, was a small green rectangle of plastic no bigger than a pack of gum.

A flash drive.

It wasn't mine.

Win.

I stepped over to the computer on my roommate's desk. The screen snapped back to life as I jiggled the mouse, a picture of Jati and a girl back in a city that looked clean and foreign enough to be his home.

I popped off the cap and plugged the memory stick into the port on the side of the computer. A window popped up asking me what I wanted to do with the new disc the computer had found. I clicked on the option for viewing files. The computer spooled up for a second before a new folder opened, thumbnails of photos tiling down the pane.

WOULD YOU LIKE TO VIEW THE SLIDE SHOW? the computer prompted me. I accepted.

The first shot was of my parents in front of our house with me.

Next a shot I'd forgotten, of the two of us at that park in Lena eating the lunch my mother had packed.

Then that shot of us at the state line, looking as tough and weird as I remembered feeling at that moment.

Then Win the morning after the church service, searching his pannier with that stupid pink flashlight.

Win on the couch with that family in Indiana who let us sleep on their backyard trampoline.

My thumb and forefinger framing the head of a giant Lincoln statue somewhere in Illinois.

Me jumping off a bridge somewhere over the Mississippi.

Win on a covered wagon in the rain outside Pepin, Wisconsin.

A shot of me from twenty yards away, streaking toward the camera, my water bottle already firing a stream toward Win.

Morgan and Effie in their kitchen, awkward, as if the camera's gaze embarrassed them.

I don't know how long I sat there as the pictures faded from one to another. The whole glorious two months unfolded before me, flooding back in a way that made me even more emotional than finding Win had.

The last picture—right after a sequence including a shot of uniformed Danielle, carrying a tray past that counter where I'd eaten just a few days ago; a shot of a fake dead cowboy in Winthrop; and a fuzzy image of a mangy, rabid coyote—was of Win.

He was sitting on the floor of Morgan's barn. I imagined he'd positioned the camera on that very crate where I'd sat when we talked. He was looking straight into the lens. In his hand he held a scrap of one of our maps—probably North Dakota, judging by the emptiness. Random letters cut from that damn bumper sticker looked tiny and crooked on the middle of the almost colorless map, creased and furry at the edges. I had to enlarge the photo to read it.

Win's message was only one word.

THANKS.

I nodded, staring at the picture a little longer before closing the window and removing the drive.

I held it in my hand, marveling that something so tiny could carry so much . . . *weight*.

I crossed to my dresser, dropping the flash drive in a plastic cup

I'd been given during orientation. I opened the top drawer and pulled out a clean pair of shorts. I hesitated before slamming it shut. I grabbed the cup and fished the drive from it. Reaching back into my drawer, I unearthed my itchiest, heaviest pair of winter socks. Mom had made me bring these, but I'd never wear them. Being warm wasn't worth that much pain.

I unfolded the ball of wool and elastic. The drive slipped quietly down into the scratchy blue, nestling in the toe. I felt it there for a second before rolling the cuffs over each other and shoving the socks back into the darkness of the drawer.

I closed it gently and stepped away, studying the dresser. It didn't look any different. Didn't look like it would burst with all the memories it held. But when I glanced in the mirror hanging over the dresser, I realized I did.

I looked like that guy from the photos. The one who knew how epic life could be. The one who knew who his friends were. The one who knew what it meant to find adventure.

I didn't need those pictures in my hands or on my wall to know that.

And I didn't need Win, either.

But it was good knowing they'd be there when I wanted a reminder.

Both of them.

Don't miss Jennifer Bradbury's
next tale of
deception and intrigue!

"Put the book down, darling," my mother said from her chair beside the mirror.

"The chapter's end is only a short way off," I replied, reaching out with my other hand to flip the page. Despite the ache in my shoulder from holding the book at arm's length so the dressmakers could work on my gown, I didn't want to give it up.

"For heaven's sake, you've read it a dozen times," Mother said, rising to snatch the book from my hand. I half lunged for it, an action answered by the jabs of a dozen pins in places sensitive enough to ensure the book was lost to me for now.

"It improves each time," I told her, letting my arms fall, the sensation of the blood rushing back into my fingertips too brief before the dressmaker nudged one elbow upward again.

"Please, miss," the woman said, gesturing at the bodice, managing to sound even more exasperated with me than Mother had.

I lifted my arms again, posing as if I were about to take

flight. According to some, I was. My debut had come, bringing with it Mother's long-awaited opportunity to parade me about in front of all of London. The dress wrapped itself around me in tucks and folds of silk the color of cream as it stands on the top of a cup of tea, waiting to be stirred in. The trim at the neckline was exquisitely wrought in lace Mother had warned me more than once not to tell Father the price of. I'd pleaded unsuccessfully to have this particular dress made from a shimmering red sari fabric my brother had sent home to me from India. Mother was firm that red was perfectly unsuitable.

She was right, of course, as she was about most everything. She was right that this color was far more appropriate for a girl making a debut, that it would allow me to fit and stand out at the same time. I wasn't sure I was ready to do either yet. And I was relatively certain I wasn't prepared to step into society as Mother's protégée. I adored my mother, but I didn't want to be her. Not yet, anyway.

"You really might at least pretend to be more diverted by all of this," she complained, turning down a corner of the page of my book before placing it on the dressing table. I fought the urge to beg her to use the scrap of lace I'd employed as a bookmark. I didn't want creases in that particular copy of *Mansfield Park*. But the damage was done. And Mother was incensed enough with me already.

"On the contrary, Mother," I said, balancing on my left foot just long enough to scratch the back of my right knee with my toe, "I find the prospect of this evening's entertainment so overwhelming that it helps to have something to occupy my mind."

Mother almost smiled. "It does promise to be an affair. I'm sure I've waited long enough before agreeing to be seen at one of these events, don't you think?"

"Never be the first or the last to adopt fashion," I said, echoing her words dutifully.

"But you *must* be the first to make an impression on our host this evening," she said, a smile beginning at the corner of her mouth. Mother had declined two earlier invitations for parties of this sort. But when this one from Lord Thomas Showalter came so fortuitously timed with my debut, Mother accepted with haste. I couldn't blame her, exactly. Lord Showalter was exactly the kind of man she or any other eager mother wanted for her daughter. He might have been the most sought-after man in all of Hyde Park, if not all of London itself. He was charming, handsome, and rich.

I rolled my eyes, whispered, *"È una verità universalmente riconosciuta che uno scapolo in possesso di una buona fortuna sia in cerca di moglie."*

"Don't mumble, dear," she ordered.

This time I slipped from Italian to Russian and spoke a bit louder. *"Все знают, что молодой человек, располагающий средствами, должен подыскивать себе жену."* I loved the way Russian insisted on tickling the back of my throat.

"Agnes." Mother's tone carried the warning for her.

I translated the line again, this time to German, so Mother might recognize it at last. *"Es ist eine allgemein anerkannte Wahrheit, daß ein Junggeselle im Besitz eines schönen Vermögens nichts dringender braucht als eine Frau."*

She stiffened, crossed her arms. "You know how it vexes me when you show off—what man will stand for that, I wonder?"

Finally, I all but shouted at her in French. *"C'est une vérité universellement reconnue, qu'un seul homme en possession d'une bonne fortune doit être dans le besoin d'une femme."*

She took a moment, narrowing her eyes to tiny slits. "It's not enough that you must cavort about in tongues that no respectable girl has any business speaking, but you must quote those books in the bargain? Honestly, Agnes."

I smiled sweetly. "I was agreeing with you," I said, "or at the very least A Lady was." I looked down at the younger of the two dressmakers. "It's from *Pride and Prejudice*," I said. "'It is a truth universally acknowledged, that a single man in possession of a good fortune, must be in want of a wife.' Have you read it?"

The girl's eyes lit up and she began to nod, but Mother cut short her reply. "Of course she's read it. Half of England has read it, which is why it's vulgar to quote it."

"Half the world has read the Bible and we quote it all the time," I teased.

"I'll pretend you didn't just compare the scribbling of a female novelist to the words of our Lord," she said. "Whatever will I do with you?"

I sighed. "Marry me off to a rich man before he sees how clever I am. And with me in this gown at this evening's most romantic of events, it appears your task is half done already."

Mother sat again, placated a bit by my apparent acquiescence to her plan. "The entertainment he has chosen is gruesome, but it will provide a stunning foil for your beauty."

We'd agreed that we would both politely decline actively participating this evening if pressed to do so. But Mother would not risk staying clear of the party outright. She was sure that Showalter was finally ready to seek a wife after several years in our London society and that if I weren't there to be seen as a candidate, my chance would be lost.

I didn't have the stomach to tell her that part of me wanted to stay here in my room and reread an A Lady novel or continue working on my Hebrew translations.

"Lady Ershing told me they do this sort of thing all the time in France. But so many of the fancies out of Europe have to be weighed against good English judgment and civility, I always say," my mother mused.

"They trim their gowns in red lace in Paris, ma'am," one of the seamstresses offered. Mother had brought the dressmakers here in order to preserve the secrecy of my gown. She couldn't bear the thought of my first debut gown being copied or seen by anyone before I'd had a chance to wear it. Her paranoia knew no bounds on this score. Already she'd been favoring the shop far from Bond Street and the prying eyes of her friends and neighbors. But bringing the dressmakers to our home was extreme even for her. She'd already arranged to do the same with the final fittings for my presentation gown, but that dress was still being pieced at the shop.

Mother jabbed a finger at the girl. "How dreadful. Just because the French do it doesn't mean we should. England is her own sovereign sensible state."

"And may we stay that way for eternity, God save the King and damn Napoleon!" I said.

Mother's gaze darkened. The two dressmakers pretended to be fascinated with the pleats. "Take care to find a way to voice your patriotism more appropriately," my mother warned.

"Yes, Mother." I sighed. But I felt the same about the mad little man across the Channel as anyone in England. Napoleon had more lives than a cat, had been the villain of the newspapers and in our household since I was a child. Before I even properly understood that he aimed for nothing less than ruling the world—and England with it—I used to spy on my brothers as they staged reenactments of the Battle of Trafalgar in the nursery.

Ten years Napoleon had haunted us. And with his most recent return from exile, the threat had gained strength anew. It was enough to make me wonder if debuting under such a shadow was at all sensible. I'd tried once to persuade Mother on this point. Her reply had been swift and certain: The very best affront we could offer the French would be to continue on with our lives as if Napoleon and his ambitions worried us not at all. Solid English tradition scoffing in the face of danger. She'd sounded as though she belonged on the floor of the House of Lords at Father's side.

Mother seemed to read my thoughts. "It is so important that you debut now, Agnes," she affirmed. "It is your duty. Our duty. To David and his compatriots, that they may know we have confidence enough in them to protect us. To those of the lower classes who need to see their betters continuing with the important traditions and rites that make ours a great nation . . . and to flout Napoleon, the little cockroach!"

I rolled my eyes. "I can hardly see how my debut will cause old Boney to flinch, Mother."

She sat up straighter, her chin lifting. "Principle, Agnes," she said gravely. "It's the principle of the matter."

"To say nothing of *your* principles," I teased. Mother had waited longer than she wished for my debut season to arrive. Her own season had resulted in a triumphant match with my father. I suppose I couldn't hold it against her that she was eager for me to find such happiness.

Mother hesitated, softened a bit, and then spoke. "Well, I have been very patient, haven't I?"

"Mother, I'm barely seventeen!" I said, falling as easily into the argument we'd been having for the last two years as I might into my own bed.

"*I* debuted at sixteen," she replied, on script. "And married your father at seventeen. Of course custom dictates a longer engagement these days. Though I think anything longer than two years is a bit absurd. . . ."

Mother suddenly sprang to her feet and worked her way in between the two dressmakers. "This pleat does not lie properly. It will not do."

"You're not so eager to marry David or Rupert off," I complained.

"David is years from being a suitable husband. And Rupert . . ." She paused, shook her head. "Even with your father's fortune, I do not know that he will have the same sense to marry so well."

"No one could marry as well as Father," I said sweetly, even meaning it.

Mother smiled, swatted at my hand. "You're a good girl, Agnes," she said. "And you'll make an excellent wife. Though I shudder to think what kind of home you'll keep." She nodded to the wallpaper. "I still can't account for those."

I smiled at the golden walls, flecked with shimmering pink cherry blossoms and snaky green dragons peeking through the branches. I'd begged Father to bring me something special when he'd gone as part of a delegation to Japan when I was nine or so. He'd brought the paper, telling Mother that the empress herself had it hanging on the walls of the throne room and that it was perfect for his dear princess.

The dull floral that had been on my wall since my grandmother's time gave way.

"I'm sure you'll be at hand to advise me," I said quietly, looking about the room at the other objects that Father had brought home during his years of travel, or that David had sent from various ports while at sea. The pointy little slippers from Turkey, the delicate toy drum from the Indies, and the dozens of books in various languages, some of which I'd managed to read, others still waiting to be unlocked.

Mother looked at me. "Lord Showalter's tastes do run quite the same direction as yours."

It was true. I'd been to Showalter's twice before, and the house was chockablock with curiosities, the bulk of which had been ferried over from Egypt. Nothing went together. Strolling through his sitting room was like rummaging through the world's attic, so varied and odd was the collection of items he possessed and displayed. He even had a small golden idol shaped like a bird on his mantelpiece.

"Perhaps you'll even be so kind as to decorate our entire house so that I might have time to concentrate on my studies?"

Mother shook her head. "Education is for children. And you've already had far more than your share. I let your father keep finding those language tutors for you, but there comes a time when every girl must step out of the schoolroom and into the life that awaits her." She held my eye. "And that time for you is come at last!"

At this, the seamstresses stepped away and looked to

Mother. She circled round me, studying every stitch and hem and pleat and ruffle and fall of fabric.

"Very good," she said finally.

I looked at myself in the mirror. Still a girl in a lovely dress, my auburn hair pinned back, waiting for Clarisse to do with it what only she could.

But what that girl in the mirror felt surprised me. I'd spent months arguing with Mother about allowing me to continue my studies, pleading with Father to convince her to delay my debut. And yet, in this dress . . .

I looked beautiful. How odd a sensation. Mother was beautiful. I was not. And yet in the dress I looked like a girl ready to make her debut, a girl who belonged at a party, or a coronation or something important. And then an even odder shiver ran through me: I wanted to see what could happen at parties and dinners for a girl dressed like I was. At least it would be something new, possibly exciting, even if it was a quick step into the rest of my life.

Suddenly all of me couldn't wait to wear this dress tonight.

Mother must have noticed the change.

"You wear it well," she said.

And for once I could not argue.

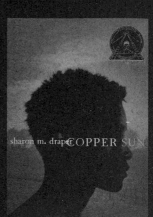

Life is hard enough without struggling to hold your family together.

"A glowing book ... An enthralling journey to a gratifying end."
— *New York Times Book Review*, on *Homecoming*

Newbery Medal Winner   Newbery Honor Book

How

do you

navigate

the

uncertain

space

where

science

and

morality

collide?

Praise for *Genesis Alpha*:

"An adrenaline-charged thriller. . . . dark, dangerous, and utterly riveting." —Kenneth Oppel, Michael L. Printz Honor–winning author of *Airborn*

Praise for *Nobel Genes*:

"Clever, intriguing, and captivating. I read it in one sitting and will be thinking about it for a long time. . . . I loved it."

—James Dashner, author of *The Maze Runner*

EBOOK EDITIONS ALSO AVAILABLE
From Atheneum Books for Young Readers
TEEN.SimonandSchuster.com